Praise for *Drinking from Graveyard Wells*

"*Drinking from Graveyard Wells* is unlike any story collection you've read or will read. These wonderful, vibrant, and beautifully executed stories of life, death, and the cultural ties forged in migration have the uncanny ability to render the world we live in more intimate and mysterious than we often imagine. A striking and original debut."
— Dinaw Mengestu, author of *All Our Names*, *The Beautiful Things that Heaven Bears*, and *How to Read the Air*

"In a set of short stories that skirt the surreal, the supernatural, and the mundane, Yvette Lisa Ndlovu invites readers into a look at life in Zimbabwe—past, present, and beyond. *Drinking from Graveyard Wells* is as mesmerizing and magical as it is unflinchingly real in its reflections, which pose questions at once personal and universal in their implications. These tales will stay with me, perhaps even haunt me, for some time to come!"
— P. Djèlí Clark, author of *A Master of Djinn* and *Ring Shout*

"Ndlovu's stunning stories drawn from Zimbabwean and African legend poise poignant questions on history, identity, and nationhood. This is a collection by a supremely gifted writer committed to preserving and reinventing ancient folktales to weave a modern lore. She deserves nothing but the highest praise."
— T. L. Huchu, author of *The Hairdresser of Harare* and *The Library of the Dead*

"Ndlovu's tragicomic, sad, bold, and big-hearted *Drinking from Graveyard Wells* announces the arrival of a major talent. Ndlovu's realism, both magic and hyper, spins around a central truth: amid collective peril, we need storytellers like Ndlovu all the more, those who might help spirit us into some semblance of our collective tomorrow."
— Edie Meidav, author of *Kingdom of the Young*

"What a trenchant and powerful collection! These big-hearted stories offer a heady cocktail of history, myth, and realism that delights and edifies, etching women's multicultural histories in a fresh and tender light. Ndlovu writes with sparkling wit and a keen eye for the everyday. Brimming with wisdom and intelligence, *Drinking from Graveyard Wells* heralds a wonderful new talent."

—Novuyo Rosa Tshuma, author of *House of Stone* and *I Dream America*

Drinking from Graveyard Wells

DRINKING
from
GRAVEYARD WELLS

stories

Yvette Lisa Ndlovu

UNIVERSITY PRESS OF KENTUCKY

Scholarly publisher for the Commonwealth, serving Bellarmine University,
Berea College, Centre College of Kentucky, Eastern Kentucky University,
The Filson Historical Society, Georgetown College, Kentucky Historical Society,
Kentucky State University, Morehead State University, Murray State University,
Northern Kentucky University, Spalding University, Transylvania University,
University of Kentucky, University of Louisville, University of Pikeville, and
Western Kentucky University.
All rights reserved.

Editorial and Sales Offices: The University Press of Kentucky
663 South Limestone Street, Lexington, Kentucky 40508-4008
www.kentuckypress.com

This is a work of fiction. The characters, places, and events are either drawn
from the author's imagination or used fictitiously. Any resemblance of fictional
characters to actual living persons is entirely coincidental.

Library of Congress Cataloging-in-Publication Data

Names: Ndlovu, Yvette Lisa, author.
Title: Drinking from graveyard wells : stories / Yvette Lisa Ndlovu.
Description: Lexington : The University Press of Kentucky, 2023.
Identifiers: LCCN 2022043823 | ISBN 9780813196978 (hardcover) | ISBN
    9780813196992 (pdf) | ISBN 9780813196985 (epub)
Subjects: LCGFT: Short stories.
Classification: LCC PR9390.9.N4387 D75 2023 | DDC 823.92—dc23/eng/20220912
LC record available at https://lccn.loc.gov/2022043823

Member of the Association
of University Presses

To my sister, Stacy, for being my first reader, role model, and rock.

And to my father, Stephen, the first storyteller in my life, who nurtured my love of reading with an unwavering belief in my impossible dreams and the magic of these stories to grow wings to carry me beyond.

Contents

Red Cloth, White Giraffe

On the day I die, my husband ties a red cloth on our gate. His hands are shaking. The cloth is from my favorite doek, the one that always looked like a rose when I tied it around my head on special occasions. He keeps the gates open for mourners to trickle in. The women wear black doeks, the strands of their hair tucked behind the thick cloth.

"Beauty has no place at a funeral!" Tete Saru screams at any woman who arrives uncovered. She never explains why the dead consider a woman's hair disrespectful.

Wails and glum hymns ricochet through the house in the twilight. The red cloth marks the commencement of the all-night vigils that happen every night until I am to be buried.

There are too many people to fit into the house, so they remove the sofas from the living room and some people sit on the hardwood flooring. The sofas are carried outside, where other family members crowd around a fire, the flames casting dancing shadows. The fire burns every night before the burial. The higher the smoke rises into the air, the higher my prospects of securing a good spot amongst the ancestors.

At the first vigil, my relatives and friends argue about how the red cloth tradition started. Disputing the fabric's origins provides a welcome distraction from the boiled cabbage swimming lifelessly on their plates. As my tete likes to remind us, eating meat at a funeral is akin to spitting in the deceased's face.

"If you cannot forgo the luxury of meat, oil, and spice, how could you say you loved the deceased?" Tete Saru says.

Tete is in charge of inspecting the food. She urges the varoora who'd been assigned cooking duties to pour bowls and bowls of salt into the big black pots of boiling cabbage for an extra measure of misery. Funerals taste like tears and seawater.

"The red cloth has always been our culture," a cousin says. He is an eager-eyed university student studying African History. "It signals to the community that a passing has occurred and a family is in mourning. It invites anyone, regardless of whether they knew the deceased or not, to come to pay their respects. It's ubuntu. Even in death, I am since we are, and since we are, therefore I am."

I wish I could smack him for sounding like a PhD dissertation and remind him of the times he ate sand, played nqobe, and did armpit farts.

"Fool!" says Sekuru Givemore, an aged uncle who'd fought in the war. "The freedom fighters during the liberation struggle started it. The white Africans, those bloody Rhodesians"—he spat on the ground after saying "Rhodesians," as if to rid himself of the colonists along with the phlegm that had built up in his throat—"were so afraid of a revolution that they made it illegal for more than five black people who weren't from the same household to meet under one roof. This made it complicated to bury our dead. An African must have a funeral as big as a wedding, or no funeral at all."

"But—"

"The Rhodesians allowed funerals to happen if households would put a marker on their gates that a funeral was occurring, so that the Rhodesian Police wouldn't disturb them as they patrolled," my sekuru says. "That marker was the red cloth."

"But—"

"Listen to your elders. The freedom fighters started meeting and plotting at funerals, and the Rhodesians were none the wiser. They never inspected a house with a red cloth on the gate. Thought they were clever, those bloody shits. That's how we beat them."

Sekuru laughs and throws a fist in the air. He starts coughing. My cousin has to slap him on the back to stop him from choking.

"It was her favorite headscarf," my husband murmurs, but he is drowned out by another origin story.

Only Tete hears him. Her usually tough demeanor softens, and she whispers the words, "Don't worry. We will find a way to bury her."

The first day of being dead is a lot like sleep paralysis. I can see and hear everything around me but somehow I can't tell my legs to move, can't will my chest to rise or fight the pull of gravity. At first my spirit doesn't register that its home is gone and that I must leave. I try to breathe life into the cells and jolt the heart to beat one last time. No matter how much I slap my limbs and try to pry open my eyelids, nothing moves at my command.

I remember Tete explaining death to me many years ago over a pot of cabbage. I was twelve, and it was my first funeral. My mother's funeral.

"Westerners will tell you that funerals are for the living, not the dead, but that's not how it works for us," Tete Saru had said.

"What do you mean, Auntie?" I asked.

"Death is not the end. It is the beginning of another long journey," she said.

She gestured for the varoora sweating over large black pots to drown the cabbage in more boiling water. The cabbage slowly turned from green to white.

"Soon you will graduate from primary school and go to high school. You will get a certificate from your school that tells the high school that you are ready for secondary education. You cannot go to high school without a certificate from your primary school. Think of death as part of a graduation ceremony at the end of mastering a long life. It is the certificate God gives you to open the gates to be with the ancestors. A spirit cannot proceed without this certificate."

When the cabbage was sufficiently devoid of color, Tete Saru nodded her head in approval. It was ready to be served.

"One cannot skip that process," Tete said, helping the cooks dump the soaked cabbage into plates and bowls. "You must crawl before you walk, and so the dead must be buried before they can advance to the after. The only problem with this process is that your family is in charge of securing your passage."

My auntie's words flood back to me as I lie in the mortuary unclaimed. Everything encasing me breaks down on a slab of steel. I yearn for a casket and fresh earth to cover me; but the dead, like newborns, are subject to the goodwill of others. My family will not bury me. The longer I stay in the mortuary, the more the gates recede.

When you're dead, all you're left with is your own thoughts. There is no body to distract you from yourself and no drink to fill the belly to quiet the musing. I lie in the cold that I cannot feel and think of how the end of flesh comes with an impatience, a call to journey to another world. At nine months a fetus yearns to break the barrier between the womb and a new world. I wonder if I will announce my arrival on the other side crying, too.

The third day of being dead, the sleep paralysis loosens.

The incandescent lightbulbs flicker on and off as the mortician stands over a table, working on a new body. He has the excitement and pride of a painter at a gallery showing. He likes to play with the pretty girls, girls who would never have breathed in his direction when they lived. At least other girls' families collected them quickly.

When his fingers linger too long on the new arrival, I fight against the last hold my body has on my spirit. Something unlocks. My spirit yawns and stretches as it leaves its cage. Before I can register this new feeling, this new way of being, I hurtle towards the mortician. He yelps in surprise as his needles, scalpels, and pointy scissors fly at him. He bellows as he bleeds on the floor. I do not look back.

Newborns suck on their toes and thumbs. They don't know what else to do in this new realm and body. I test out my new being by whipping through doors and walls. I escape from the building's sterile walls and fly to a school playground. The children marvel at the empty swing rocking back and forth. I soon grow bored and float above the city, searching for a place to go. I see a gate with a red ribbon and race towards it.

Everyone is curious to know if they will get to attend their own funeral, but I want to know what it's like to attend the funeral of another, as a spirit. It's the last day of a vigil. Whoever has died will be buried tomorrow. The body rests in a coffin in the living room, sleeping one last time in its home before burial. The spirit stands over the open coffin, staring at what she once was.

"You're . . . dead . . . too." I try to get used to my new voice. It sounds like when the wind moans on a stormy night. "What's your name?"

The spirit doesn't look up. She continues to stare at her body, longing for the warmth of being alive.

"Maya."

"Why are you upset?" I say, irritated. "At least your family is burying you!"

Her casket is completely gold. The inside has a soft white velvet lining.

"I won't be able to cross the gates to the after," Maya says. She points at herself in the coffin. She is wearing a pretty floral dress. That's when I notice that she has one leg.

"I lost my leg in the car accident. I will never become an ancestor." She weeps bitterly.

"A woman cannot proceed to the after without being whole," I say. "That's what Tete Saru told me."

When I still had breath, I thought life was unfair, but death is a different kind of unfair. Spirits, especially female spirits, can be barred from the after for anything. Even women who donate their organs are not considered "whole" and cannot pass through the gates.

I fly away from the damned spirit towards home. Death is supposed to provide rest. But for Maya and me, it is just another system whose boot we live under. I throw birds at car windshields and laugh. I enter traffic lights and play with the pretty colors. I can't tell if I like amber or green more. I avoid red. Car horns bellow as drivers swerve to avoid each other's bumpers.

I remember the day before I died, my husband drove me to the hospital. We drove down the street lined with purple-flowered jacaranda trees as we always did. Suddenly my husband braked, nearly veering off the road. Out of nowhere a giraffe ran across the crosswalk and onto the street opposite Edgar's department store. The shoppers inside pointed at the marvel outside. The Chipangali Wildlife Orphanage is only ten kilometers out of town, so it was nothing new for an animal to escape and make its way into rush hour traffic, blinded and scared by headlights. This giraffe in particular wasn't spotted. It was completely white, as if it had been thrown into my auntie's cabbage pot. A red tuft of fur clung to the base of its long neck. I don't know why, but my hands went to the red doek tied over my hair.

"I don't think I should go to the hospital," I said.

"You are starting to sound like Tete Saru," my husband said, shaking his head. "It's rare, so what?"

"If something unexpected crosses a path you take every day," I insisted, "you must turn back."

"If everyone did that, no one would leave their homes," my husband said, driving on.

Hours later the giraffe was shot, tranquilized, and airlifted back to Chipangali.

My death, like my life, was not exciting; just an incident beyond my control. Born with stubborn kidneys, I endured three weekly hospital visits for four hours. I would greet the nurse in her starched white uniform and white stockings. She would make a joke about seeing me more often than her own husband. She would weigh me, take my temperature and blood pressure, poke a needle or two and a colony of tubes into my arms. I would sit by the dialysis machine as the blood flowed into and out of my body until it was time to go home.

Kidney failure.

What a weird expression. As if my organs were students in a class competing for gold stars. My kidneys were the student that never applied himself, the student that cut class and never dreamed beyond an F.

The stats show that with dialysis treatment, patients can live a long, healthy life. These stats didn't account for the fact that I lived in Zimbabwe. The machines are old, and the doctors and nurses were on a four-month strike before I passed. The friendly nurse left for Britain or America. I was the number, the variable the smart people didn't account for in their studies, and so I died.

"Gone too soon" is what they call spirits like mine. Spirits that are most likely to get hung up on the injustices of their lives and become ngozi in death. "The dead must move on as the living do" is what I was taught when I was young. I don't know if I believe in that anymore.

When I rush through my home's gates, I find my husband pleading, begging my family to see reason.

"The mortuary fees are piling up," he says. "How long will you keep her away from joining the ancestors?"

The men from my family do not soften.

"If you want to bury her," they say, "finish paying for her lobola."

"I do not have the money," my husband says.

"She will not be buried until you do," my family says, unwavering.

A woman has two weddings. The lobola and the white. On the morning of my lobola ceremony, a delegation from my future husband's family made up of his brothers, uncles, and father came knocking on our gate. My father did not let them in.

"We don't want to seem too eager," he said, his face buried behind a newspaper. He turned the page with a flourish.

My husband's family stayed outside the gates all morning waiting for an invitation to come inside. I paced back and forth in my room, anxious that they would get tired, give up, and go. I remembered reading an article in the *Chronicle* about a groom who had been kept waiting outside his bride's home for two hours and was hit by a drunk driver who drove onto the curb. The bride price money was still in his pocket. It was either blood money or the bride was cursed, everyone in the city mused. I didn't want to be called a cursed bride.

I repeatedly texted my husband, who was then my boyfriend, that I loved him. He sent back hearts and said I was worth the wait. I bit my nails and waited. I tried to push away the nagging question in my mind. Why must my lover pay the men in my family for their blessing? Loving me came with an invoice, a big invoice.

A little after one o'clock my father finally let them in. I was to stay in my room; women weren't allowed at the negotiation table. I pressed my ear to the door.

"Our daughter is educated, she got her degree abroad," an uncle was saying. "This means your children will be smart and she can help them with the homework."

"She is beautiful, not too dark," another uncle chimed in.

"She also knows how to cook," my father said. "This meal you are eating. She prepared it all by herself!"

I heard murmurs of approval from the other side.

"We cannot let such a good daughter go away for nothing."

The men in my family continued to list all the metrics that calculated my value. The men from my boyfriend's family repeatedly tried to lower the price, but my family would not allow for a discount. Then came a moment of silence. I knew my father was scribbling down a figure on the paper and would slide the paper over to the other side. This ensured that no eavesdropping women heard the figure.

Halfway through the negotiations, my cousin came to fetch me. My heart pounded in my chest as I entered the dining room. I kept my expression demure, head bowed, not meeting anyone's eyes.

"Is this the woman you have come to collect?" my father asked my boyfriend.

I considered this mandatory part of the ritual silly. Who else would he have come for? I didn't have sisters.

"Yes," my boyfriend said, keenly.

"Do you know this man?" my father asked me.

I lifted my gaze to my boyfriend and smiled.

His uncles admired me. "A good catch," they all whispered and nodded to each other.

"Yes, I know him," I answered. Tete Saru had told me before not to answer the question too fast. I wasn't supposed to be too eager.

"Then the bride price is settled," my father said. Everyone let out a sigh of relief. My father poured whiskey and beer to celebrate.

I wonder how much my husband paid for me. I wasn't allowed to know the figure. Knowing brought bad luck upon the marriage.

In the old days lobola was simple. A groom brought a bag of maize, a piece of jewelry, or a gardening hoe as a token of appreciation to the bride's family. Now most grooms beg to pay in installments. My husband has been paying for me for years and is nowhere near done clearing the bill. I died before he finished paying for my lobola. Now my family put the debt collector's cap on and demanded he pay up, or my body would rot in the mortuary. They withheld their blessing for a funeral until every cent of my bride price was paid.

My husband tosses and turns at night until he finds a restless sleep. I stand over the bed and climb to my side. I peer at him, my face so close to his that he shivers. Earlier, I entered a stray cat and made it go mad. That's when I discovered that spirits could enter anything alive, inhabit its flesh momentarily. I wonder what lurks inside.

I slip into him through the nose and land in his dreams. Here, I am still alive. This is our first date, brought together by the magic of algorithms and a swipe right. We are the only two Zimbabwean students abroad in our year, both homesick to hear our own language and taste home in a faraway place. Outside the African restaurant he greets me and we hug. Instead of saying hello, I whisper,

"Bury me."

Suddenly his spirit ejects me from his body. Human bodies are harder to inhabit. You cannot just go into someone else's house and claim it as your own.

When my husband wakes up, he polishes his shoes and visits the loan sharks. When he returns, he tosses a briefcase full of cash at my father and uncles.

"Here is the rest of her bride price," my husband says.

"We can bury her tomorrow," my father announces.

Throughout our marriage, my husband refused to tell me how much he owed, refused to tell me how much my family had bartered me for. I finally know the figure. The money is divided between my father and my uncles. I watch them smell the fresh notes and stuff them hungrily in their pockets.

It doesn't take much to piss off a spirit. I watch my uncles plan out how they will spend the money. Some will splurge on a trip to Cape Town, and others will use it to spoil their Brazilian-weave-loving "small houses" with new handbags and phones. Men who've never contributed anything to my life are now thousands of dollars richer. It was Tete Saru who took care of me when my mom died. In all the memories of significant moments in my life, it is my auntie's presence that I can recall. Yet she does not get a cent of the bride price. If anyone deserves payment, it's her.

Maya appears on the day of my burial. We both watch as they lower the coffin into the ground. The arched gates to the after appear above the open grave, aglow in sunlight. Maya shades her face with a hand, cowering before the luminous gates. I can see the longing in her eyes. I should feel that longing too. All I feel in this moment is rage.

An uncle in a shiny new suit stands over my grave with a shovelful of dirt. The dirt spills across the casket. My husband shakes with anger as another shovelful hits my casket.

"You should go now," Maya says. "The gates will shut when the last bit of earth covers your coffin."

Tete Saru rocks herself back and forth as my grave begins to fill. A single tear rolls down her cheek. I've never seen her cry at funerals. Her eyes fix on the spot where the gates hover, as if she can see them.

I know what I must do, but I cannot move, cannot bring myself to enter through the gates as if I am at peace.

"I cannot," I whisper.

"You need to go or you will be stuck here," Maya says.

"I will not!" I shout.

The ground shakes, the headstones around us rattle. The money in my uncles' pockets becomes a leash that pulls them towards the hole in the ground. They try to fight against the force as the earth beneath them gives way. One by one, they fall into the grave.

"If you touch grave soil before you die," I say, "you become next."

I curse all my greedy uncles. Back home, the red cloth by the gate burns. The gates recede beyond my reach.

I become an avenging spirit.

I become a ngozi.

My anger leads me to Chipangali. Ngozi haunt particular places. I don't know why the Wildlife Orphanage is where I end up. Maya follows me here. As someone who died on a road, she has nowhere else to go. We wander down the winding dust roads the tour guides use for safari tours. A tour van drives through me as foreign tourists point at the zebras and wildebeest walking by. They *ooh* and *aah* at the water hole where a herd of elephants are rolling around in the mud. I know all the animals see us. A baby elephant lifts its trunk and waves at me. Its mother leads it away.

That's when I see it again. The white giraffe. It emerges from behind the bushes. It is no longer completely white. A huge gash is on its neck, red blood oozing out. I know, like me, the white giraffe is dead. Killed by trophy hunters. Such a beautiful creature can never last long in the world. I approach and stroke it. The white giraffe bends down to rub its head against mine.

"It's okay," I say to the giraffe. "You've got me now. Let's go find those who hurt you."

I climb on its back. When it rises again, I am so high off the ground I can see everything.

Second Place Is the First Loser

"Almost doesn't fill a bowl." That's what I expected Baba to say to me once he found out the truth. Either that or "Second place is the first loser." His favorite sayings crossed my mind as the plane touched down in Bulawayo. The last time he'd said the words out loud to me was six years ago. I was twelve, and we were playing tsoro yematatu. Before I could make my winning move, Baba made a calculated one. I threw my hands up. I had almost won. "Almost doesn't fill a bowl," he said, taking away the six pieces from the board. You don't get partial credit for failure.

Baba had hand-carved the board when he was a little boy. It was his most prized possession. The board was a triangle with a cross carved inside it. This gave us seven possible points to put our pieces. There were six pieces in total, and winning the game meant placing them three-in-a-row. "Rematch?" said Baba, a childlike joy in his eyes. "What color pieces do you want this time?" But I pushed back against playing this stupid village game all the time. I told him that I would be better off playing a more sophisticated board game like chess, not this African thing. Baba reminded me that there was plenty you could learn from this African thing. That tsoro yematatu was a game of strategy and mathematics, and that I needed to think fast, figure out the probability that my opponent would make a certain move and block it beforehand.

"I can do that with chess," I said, folding my arms. "What if people at school find out I play this village game? Everyone will laugh at me."

I never played tsoro yematatu again after that.

I shook the memory away as we walked down the stairs of the South African Airlines plane and onto the tarmac of Joshua Nkomo International Airport.

"I'm so excited," Chad said into his iPhone camera.

He was making a video for his YouTube channel. It had over 50,000 subscribers so far, and his end-of-the-year goal was to reach a million viewers. He told his viewers that this was his first time in Africa, drawing out the continent's name as if it were some wild creature, a new species just waiting to be tamed and domesticated.

When he'd first introduced himself as Chad during an Orientation Week icebreaker at Cornell, I'd remarked, "Chad? Like the country?" He and everyone else in the group had stared at me blankly.

I was still bitter that Chad had gotten a majority of the votes to be president of the International Students Union, a position I had campaigned for for nearly a year. Chad wasn't even an international student, but his blond hair and hip charm had won over everyone. Second place is the first loser.

"I'm out here with my friend from college, Dineo," Chad said. "Say hi to everyone, Dinny!"

Chad shoved the camera in my face and I flashed some teeth. I hoped he wasn't going to have that camera on all the time. I could imagine the horror on my father's face at being recorded.

Chad rambled on about how we'd flown from the resort town of Victoria Falls to my hometown, Bulawayo. He ran his fingers through his blond hair and took a deep breath. "Even the air smells fresher here," he said.

I rolled my eyes. Airport air was definitely not fresher, but I let Chad enjoy being an American tourist.

Baba picked us up in his white Isuzu. He seemed older, weighed down. I knew things in the country were getting worse. Inflation kept rising and rising, and there were projections that soon we'd be resorting to barter and trade as currency. Being away from home for a year, I hadn't noticed this change in Baba through our WhatsApp video calls. He'd been cheerful as always when we chatted.

"Welcome to the City of Kings," Baba said to Chad.

Chad thanked my father for hosting. "I've always wanted to visit Africa," Chad said. "How do you say 'thank you' in the local language?"

His camera was pointed outside the car window. There was nothing fascinating on the road from the airport into town, but Chad stared wide-eyed and repeated the words "so cool" several times. Baba and I exchanged a look.

"It's 'ngiyabonga,'" Baba said. I didn't detect any annoyance in his voice. My father was too well-mannered to ever be rude to a guest. "So how was your first year at Cornell?"

"Ni–gee–bonga," Chad said, butchering the word. He told Baba about how he had chosen to live in the international students dorm because he wanted to "widen his horizons" and that's how he had met me and other "diverse people."

"Dineo, you told me you were campaigning to be president of the International Students Union. How did that go?" Baba asked.

"I'm president," Chad blurted out before quickly adding, "but Dineo worked so hard that I made her Diversity Chair."

Baba didn't respond. Over the silence I could almost hear him say, second place is the first loser.

Our car approached the robots. Where there should have been a red, amber, or green light was completely black. During the power cuts, the robots stopped working.

Chad watched fascinated, leaning forward from the backseat to see everything up ahead. He asked, how does traffic stay orderly without working traffic lights?

"Traffic lights? You mean the robots?" Baba said. "Those haven't been working for a while. I've even forgotten what their purpose is."

"Zimbabweans call traffic lights robots," Chad said into the camera. "That's so cute."

I wanted the leather seats to swallow me whole.

"It's amazing that all the cars aren't hitting each other," Chad said.

"Same logic as an all-way stop," Baba said patiently. "We give each other turns depending on who arrived at the intersection first."

We'd just passed the dead robots safely when suddenly the Isuzu's engine coughed and the car slowed to a stop. We all got out and stood by the front bumper. When Baba opened the hood, smoke plumed out. It made my eyes tear up, and Chad coughed until he was red in the face. Baba grumbled about how he should have taken the hunk of metal to a garage but their prices kept rising.

Great, this is just what I needed, I thought, *Chad recording "a car breakdown in Africa" for all his new followers to see.*

"Should we call a taxi?" Chad said. He was capturing the smoke coming out of the car like it was a rare butterfly he just spotted.

"Sure sure. I will call an African taxi," Baba said, chuckling. "Get your bags out of the car, kids."

I wanted to die when Baba began hailing cars that were going in our direction. I wanted to sink into the ground with embarrassment. Everything I loathed about this place was on full display for the whole world to see.

"We're hitchhiking?" Chad said, uncertainly. "Is that . . . you know . . . safe?"

"It's not hitchhiking," Baba said. "It's a lift."

"A what?" Chad said.

"We call it a lift or a private car," Baba said.

My father explained how our transportation system was unreliable, especially with this inflation going on. Chad nodded in fascination as Baba described how people just hailed a car and someone going in the same direction would pick them up and drop them off for a small tip as a thank-you.

"I've used my car as a lift sometimes too," Baba said.

"So it's kind of an informal community ride-sharing service?" Chad said. He put his camera down for the first time since we'd landed. He scratched his chin, deep in thought. This was the thoughtful Chad I saw in classes at Cornell. The Chad who could tackle a problem set by just staring it down.

"When you get into a stranger's car, though," he said, "aren't you afraid of, like, serial killers?"

"There are no serial killers here," Baba said. "Unless you count the government." Baba laughed out loud at his own joke.

A Honda Fit stopped in front of us. A friendly old man was behind the wheel and waved at us. We loaded our luggage into the boot and squeezed into the small car. Chad took out his camera again.

"This is called a lift," he said into the camera. "It's a Zimbabwean ride-share."

Chad wouldn't shut up about lifts all the next day. I didn't know why he was so fascinated by them. It was embarrassing that my town's transportation system was so unreliable that we had to catch a lift everywhere most of the time. Yet Chad seemed to think it was some bright idea. He rambled on about it at dinner.

"That was so cool!" Chad said. "I still can't believe what a brilliant idea it is. This could revolutionize the transport industry."

"It would be nice if we had a subway," I said, throwing a ball of sadza into my mouth. "Then we wouldn't have to rely on strangers to get around."

"Come on, think about it, Dinny," Chad said. His eyes were bright. "This could be the Amazon of driving. Lifts let drivers leverage all the unused inventory that they're carrying in their cars."

"And what's this unused inventory?" I said, stifling a yawn. My okra stew was more interesting than this conversation.

"Empty seats!" Chad said. "Think about it, Dinny! Zimbabwe is sitting on the biggest transportation innovation of our time!"

"Your words are falling on closed ears," Baba said. "Dineo will never see all that her country has to offer."

"There is no innovation here," I said. "Just corruption, inflation, and misery."

Chad sighed and shook his head. He looked at me as if I were lost. It was the look Baba gave me regularly. After dinner Chad continued to ask a million questions about the logistics of lifts as we sat in the living room. The boy was obsessed.

So are there lifts in every city in this country?

Do the majority of Zimbabweans trust lift drivers?

Has anyone tried to formalize the service? You know, like, turn it into a company?

I laughed sharply, almost choking on my own spit. I concluded that the African heat had turned Chad's brain to marshmallow for him to think that lifts were even an idea worth turning into a company.

Chad rambled on about the idea until I resorted to bringing up his YouTube channel to get him to talk about something else.

"I finished editing the vlog of us in Victoria Falls," he said, opening his laptop. "I'm going to upload it tonight. Want to see?"

Baba and I huddled behind Chad and peered at the video on his screen.

YouTube Video

Chad signs the book at the Visitor Center and high-fives a local guide, a man three times his age. He points at a map of the gorges and traces the trail to the falls. Sometimes my shadow can be seen hovering at the bottom of the frame, but I mostly avoid the camera. The video is captioned MY SUMMER TRIP TO AFRICA: VICTORIA FALLS, ZIMBABWE, JUNE 2005.

Chad is in khaki shorts, sunglasses, and a safari hat, with a backpack strapped to his back. In his fresh tan, he is the image of zeal and youth. The hike through the rainforest plays at two times speed with a jingle in the background until Chad sees a rainbow peeking through the trees, creating pockets of light amongst the greenery.

"Whoa," he says, pointing. "We're here!"

The water gushes down the cliff with a roar. The cascade is relentless—as if the water is angry, as if a deluge isn't enough, as if it needs to tear through the land until everything is eroded. Chad's shirt is soaked by the spray. He brings his hands to his ears to muffle the sound of the torrent.

"To all the Cornellians watching," Chad screams. "This is the largest waterfall in the world."

The waterfall is so loud his voice is drowned out. Subtitles appear at the bottom of the screen.

"We may say Ithaca is gorges but this—" he says.

We walk down a bridge that arches over the gorge at two times speed again, fast-forwarding to the moment when Chad bungee-jumps down the gorge. His hands are outstretched like wings. I can almost feel the wind between his fingers. He is so confident that the rope will not snap, that everything always turns out okay.

After the bungee jump, we stand near David Livingstone's statue. The statue overlooks the falls. It has loomed over the falls for more than half a century. David Livingstone leans against a walking stick with a hand on his hip. Chad is dressed just like Livingstone.

"This is the explorer who discovered these falls." Chad says, and reads from the plaque.

He bows in appreciation before the statue.

Baba cleared his throat when the video ended. He was frowning. Chad looked at us expectantly.

"Dineo," Baba said. "Why didn't you tell our guest that David Livingstone didn't discover the falls?"

The shame that overcame me was like heartburn. The disappointed look in Baba's eyes stung. Baba was going to go into a long lecture about history again. My eyes went to the door. If I said I was still tired from the flight, maybe I could go to bed early to avoid being chewed out.

"What do you mean?" Chad asked.

"The Tonga people were already living in that area long before David Livingstone arrived," Baba said. "So how can David Livingstone have discovered the falls when people lived there?"

"I never considered that," Chad said. Color rose to his cheeks.

"Another thing that my daughter didn't tell you is that their name isn't Victoria Falls," my father said. "They are called Mosi-oa-Tunya. That's what the Tonga people named them, and that is their name."

"Mosi-oa-tunya?" Chad said, trying to feel the name with his tongue.

"When Livingstone went to the falls, he decided to name them after his Queen Victoria," my father said. "Didn't bother to ask the natives if the falls had a name, even though it was natives who'd taken him to the falls in the first place."

Chad swallowed, a lump forming at his throat, and mumbled a "Thank you for educating me."

Later, when Baba wasn't looking, he uploaded the video to You-Tube anyway.

On the fifth day in Bulawayo, there was a citywide power cut. It gave me a small joy to see Chad have a near breakdown when both his laptop and phone ran out of battery. I smirked when he sighed yet again and stared longingly at his phone's black screen. We could have gone out, but he didn't want to go anywhere if he couldn't record it, so we stayed at home all day waiting for the electricity to come back.

When the sun set, Baba lit a candle and we sat in the dark, the faint light flickering.

Suddenly Chad pointed at the glass cabinet in the corner. "What's that wooden thing in there?" Chad said. "Is that a board game?"

I narrowed my eyes. He was pointing at that wretched game tsoro yematatu.

"It's just a village game," I said. "Don't bother with it. Why don't we play some chess?"

"No way," Chad said. "That looks way more interesting than chess."

Baba retrieved the tsoro yematatu board and pieces from the display. He blew off the dust that had settled on the board.

"I have no one to play with," he said sadly. "So it has been sitting in the display for years."

"I'll play with you!" Chad said.

Baba's mouth formed an O. It was like he couldn't believe his ears. "You want to play this?" he said, holding up the board as if it were a mist that would fade away if he didn't hold it carefully.

"Of course, why not?" Chad said.

I could see the joy returning to Baba's eyes in that instant. A new energy had found its way back into my baba's body as he cleared the coffee table and set the board down. He gave Chad the white pieces and kept the black pieces for himself.

Baba explained the rules of the game to Chad just as he had explained them to me so long ago:

You win by being the first to create a three-in-a-row with your pieces.

A piece can be moved by moving one space per turn onto a vacant point following the pattern on the board.

Or a piece can be moved by jumping over another piece adjacent to it. The jump must be in a straight line and follow the pattern on the board. Unlike most board games, there are no captures in this game.

Baba demonstrated how to make a winning move. Chad gave him a high-five. Baba sounded so excited as he spoke, as if his soul were awakening. I had never seen him this happy since I stopped playing with him. Baba and Chad both concentrated on their next move, treating each move as the most serious decision they ever had to make. They did not rush to move their pieces. Their faces did not betray their emotions. Their moves were precise and calculated. I was shocked by how quickly Chad picked up the game, as if he'd been playing it his whole life.

The game lasted a long time. Chad won.

The Herald
Harare, Zimbabwe
14 Oct 2014

US Company Profits off Zim Concept

United States company Lyft is dominating the ride-sharing market and plans to go global. The ride-sharing service offers an affordable alternative to taxis, all with the click of a button. Chad Zimmerman, Lyft's founder, told journalists at a press conference in San Francisco in June that the idea of starting a ride-sharing company came from Zimbabwe, where car-sharing is commonplace.

"They are called 'lifts' in Zimbabwe," Zimmerman said. "Despite the lack of a public transportation system, Zimbabweans are able to get around efficiently thanks to a vibrant ride-sharing movement."

After travelling to Zimbabwe, Zimmerman launched Zimride, which was geared towards longer trips between US cities, in 2007 at Cornell University in New York State. Six months later, the service had signed up 20 percent of the campus.

"A lot of people think that the name Zimride was taken from my name," said Zimmerman, "but it was in fact adopted from the Zimbabwean concept of community car-sharing."

The ShortLine bus stopped at the grimy Port Authority Bus Terminal in Manhattan and I dragged my suitcase, the only thing to my name, through the terminal, looking out for the signs to the subway. I wasn't looking forward to the long ride to JFK Airport. I passed an electronic message board with the time. *June 30, 2014, 2:00:00.* I overheard two tourists passing by.

"We can take a Lyft to the hotel," one tourist said. "Then walk around for the rest of the afternoon."

His partner took out his phone and tapped on the screen. "Sweet," he said. "It will be here in five minutes."

I froze at the word *Lyft*.

I pulled my phone from my pocket and stared at the pink logo. I had downloaded the app earlier in the year and never used it. Sometimes I would wake up in the middle of the night and stare at it. I even avoided social engagements because I knew people would want to carpool afterward. I tried to avoid Lyfts, but they were everywhere, on everyone's lips and on every car windshield.

My finger shook as I tapped the screen to open the app for the first time. A map filled my screen with little icons of moving cars.

Where are you going?

I typed in "JFK Airport" and selected my terminal. A driver was ready to pick me up in four minutes.

The driver pulled up in a Honda CR-V and put my suitcase in his trunk. He looked like he was in his sixties. He offered me water and an outlet to charge my phone. The car smelled like Febreze. The GPS directed us in a nasal accent.

My throat went dry as soon as I stepped into the car. Lifts at home were filled with conversations about the economy, and prayers and gospel music about how things will get better. This car was cold and smelled too sweet. When the GPS announced which street we should turn into, it sounded like it was laughing at me.

"Where are you flying to, young lady?" the driver said.

"Zimbabwe," I said.

I felt something constrict in my heart. I'd come to America with dreams and I was leaving with only a suitcase.

"That's a long way from here!" he exclaimed. "I've never been to Africa. Would love to go. Do they have Lyfts over there in Africa? Probably not, right?"

I squeezed my thigh before I answered. I wanted to scream at him but forced a polite smile. I could tell he was watching me through the rearview mirror. He was probably going to go home and tell his loved ones the highlight of his day was picking up an African.

"We have lifts," I said.

"Wow, who would have thought," he said.

The Lyft driver mentioned that he was a veteran. He had been one of the first drivers to sign up when Lyft started. "If it wasn't for Lyft," he said, "I wouldn't have enough to keep a roof over my head."

He flicked the rosary that dangled from the rearview mirror. New York's skyscrapers seemed to close in on me.

Business Insider
22 Mar 2016

Battle of the Transportation Titans

Long before there was Uber, Chad Zimmerman traveled to Zimbabwe on a summer break in 2005. There he discovered a form of hitchhiking that shuttled people around the chaotic streets of an African city. Inspired by his discovery, he returned to the United States and launched a ride-sharing company called Zimride in 2007. In 2013 the company rebranded under the name Lyft.

Today, Lyft is a distant number two to Uber, its main competitor. Founded in 2009, Uber has innovated beyond Lyft. Uber now has its own Research & Development facility to develop autonomous cars and is expanding into food delivery service. As the company expands, however, so too have its problems. Drivers are striking all over the USA, condemning the company's predatory structure.

Both Lyft and Uber have put no effort
into providing benefits for their drivers,
and have steadily opposed all attempts to

I threw my phone across the room before finishing the *Business Insider* article. Baba, who was playing tsoro yematatu by himself, barely glanced at me. These days he talked to himself and moved the pieces on the board as if an apparition were sitting across from him.

"It's not fair. He got that idea from us," I said. "If it weren't for us, he wouldn't have that stupid company, and even Uber wouldn't have been a thing."

Baba looked up at me, his hand looming over a game piece. "I seem to recall that you laughed in his face when he proposed turning lifts into a company," he said. "You called it a stupid African thing. Just like you call this game a stupid African thing."

Pangs of guilt and regret brought me back to when Chad and I were still friends, when he was sitting on this very couch playing tsoro yematatu with my father. Now he was a millionaire and we didn't speak. Life had gone marvelously for him ever since his trip to Zimbabwe. He already had a successful company by the time he graduated. I had nothing. I came back to my corrupt country with no job prospects or hope. I sat all day in the living room applying to companies I'd never hear back from.

"Tell me, Dineo, how do you measure success?" Baba said. He made a three-in-a-row on the board and sat back. "You don't think anything is valuable until it's given to you by a white person. Now that a white person has made lifts into a company, suddenly you think it's a good idea."

I remembered my last conversation with Chad after the summer trip in 2005. It was on campus, right under the clock tower. The alma mater was chiming.

"You really need to give up this Zimride idea or whatever it is you're calling it," I'd said to him. "It's so stupid. It would never work in a developed country like America. What sane American would ride in a complete stranger's car?"

"It's sad that you can't see the innovation in your own backyard, Dinny," Chad said.

His tone was so sanctimonious, so full of pity that I shook with anger. How dare he speak to me as if I were a child? How dare he expect me to be proud of my backyard when it was people like him that had pillaged that same backyard in the first place? When it was people like him that used my backyard as a punchline?

"You're just a culture vulture masquerading as a hippie," I spat. "You're no better than that colonizer David Livingstone."

Chad flinched and stepped back as if I'd struck him. Something flashed in his eyes. I couldn't tell if his grimaces were anger, embarrassment, or sadness.

"I think it's time for us to go our separate ways," he said.

I watched his back recede into the sunset on Ho Plaza. We never spoke again after that, and the campus was big enough that we never ran into each other again.

I pushed the memory down and watched Baba start another game by himself in our living room. The overhead lights went dark. I cursed ZESA and the endless power cuts as I tried to light a candle. Each match refused to light, breaking every time I slid it against the matchbox. Baba stopped playing his game, came over, and took the matches from me. The match lit on the first try in his hands.

"Even lifts are now an import from the West," Baba said, shaking his head. His voice had a quiet I-told-you-so timbre to it. He went back to his game. He seemed so at peace playing tsoro yematatu in the dark. The truth and my own shortsightedness stung.

"You know what makes me sad?" Baba said. "Chad saw a nice thing people were doing for each other and thought—how do I make money with it? That's what makes me sad."

The rage I felt made my skin hot. I charged towards Baba and grabbed the tsoro yematatu board from the coffee table, the game pieces flying across the room. I smashed the board on the ground, and it shattered into a million pieces.

Home Became a Thing with Thorns

They take Jabu's eyes on a Tuesday morning. The snowflakes fall with an obscene tenderness outside. We are inside a sterile government building that looks like a cross between a DMV and a church. The building seems to be designed to keep any warmth out, lest the kwer-ekweres inside get comfortable. It is the kind of cold that takes hold of your bones and refuses to let go.

My friend Jabu is a painter. With a stroke of a brush, he can put rainbows to shame. He likes to paint our homeland, the beautiful blue sky we left behind when home became a thing with thorns. The naturalization priest lays a hand over Jabu's eyes, and just like that, Jabu's beautiful brown eyes vanish as if they've never existed. The spot where his eyes used to be is as smooth as an arm. Jabu collapses to the ground and retches on all fours into a plastic bin. Jabu isn't the first to vomit during a naturalization ceremony, so the priests always have those little plastic bins stationed at every corner of the building. The naturalization priest's face sours like it might if he spotted a fat rat scurrying into his kitchen. Jabu retches until there is nothing left to come out of him anymore. He dry heaves and wails for the rest of the naturalization ceremony. He can't even cry, they took his eyes.

One never knows what the naturalization priests are going to take from a kwerekwere. The only thing we do know is that they will take something that you love. I remember my conversation with Jabu before the naturalization ceremony.

"I won't be a kwerekwere anymore," he'd said, his eyes lighting up at the prospect of his dreams coming together like pieces of a puzzle to a decent life. "When I'm a citizen I will take shifts at the power plant during the day and then paint at night. I'll save up to open up my own gallery, you'll see."

"I can't wait to brag to everyone that I have a friend with a gallery," I said.

I watch Jabu on the floor now. The wretched of the earth are not meant to make art, we are supposed to be too busy surviving. The corners of the priest's mouth twitch upwards in delight at the humiliation. Another kwerekwere shown his place. Even though I too want to slump to the ground, I move towards Jabu and help him up.

"Come on, Jabu," I say. "Stop it."

I know it's cruel, but I have to be the stronger one. I can't let Jabu end up like Asha. God forbid he ends up like Asha.

"You're a citizen now!" I remind him, giving him a squeeze. "Forget your eyes. They are—were—a small price to pay."

"They . . . they took . . ." he whimpers, still unable to fully comprehend what happened, "my eyes."

"You can find other ways to make art, Jabu!" I say, pulling his hair back so he can retch some more. "Others have it worse. Please, I don't want you to end up like . . ."

Asha is—was—our friend. While we all picked up the new language and tried to iron out our old accents like pressing the wrinkles out of clothing, Asha refused to learn the new tongue. It was her form of resistance. This place would take from us anyway, Asha said, why not hold on to something. Then the naturalization priest took her language. No longer could she sing Stella Chiweshe and Leonard Dembo songs, songs that reminded us of the old weddings and parties from the homeland before everything was lost. She didn't eat for a month after she got her citizenship. We found her hanging from the ceiling on a Sunday night.

"It could be worse," I say again, trying to convince myself more than him.

The naturalization priests don't only take body parts and voices. They can take away joy, names, love, beauty, songs, laughter, family recipes, music, and so much more I shudder to think about. But that is the price of citizenship.

I take Jabu home to the two-bedroom apartment we share with four other kwerekweres, buy him a cane, and make inquiries into getting him a service dog. I will do everything in my power to ensure he lands on his feet. Our roommates know the weight of the taking, they've seen it countless times, they saw it with Asha. So they allow Jabu to have one of the rooms by himself tonight. Jabu doesn't speak. When I sing "Chirara Mwana Wangu," a lullaby my gogo used to sing to me whenever I was restless, he keens until I can't bear to hear it anymore. Perhaps if Asha were here, she would have done a better job of soothing him with song. Before I bolt out of his room, he asks me, his voice a hoarse rasp of what it once was, "What do you think they will take from you?"

His question haunts me. My naturalization ceremony is in a week. If I don't go through with the naturalization, they will send me back to the homeland. I've worked so hard just to stay here for that to be my end. Whatever the priests take from me, I will just have to live with it. I will sacrifice anything to stay here.

Protests rage in the city. People carry placards denouncing the naturalization priests. On TV, a local man with a sneer on his face shouts that if it's so bad here, then go back to where you came from. I ignore the arrogance of one who has never known what it means to have a graveyard for a home. It is the arrogance of a man with solid earth beneath his feet. But I know that the ground we stand on is quicksand pretending to be solid.

During the week, I try to forget about what's coming. I work under the table as a burner at the power plant that powers the city, harrowing work no one else wants. The power plant has five chimneys like a coal plant, the chimneys smoky eyesores that tower over the city. On my first day at work, I discovered that it isn't coal that fuels the city. In the morning, a storage truck drops off large containers from the previous week's naturalization ceremonies. Each of the containers is labelled with a date. We unload the containers and burn whatever we find inside.

My mind wanders during the burning as I toss limbs, recipes, tongues, songs, and marriage certificates into a giant furnace. The furnace burps and farts out smoke whenever I feed it something new. The furnace's heat is not comforting. When I burn, I think of butterflies. The monarch butterfly is native to this land. It cannot survive cold winters. I read somewhere that it can travel as far as 3,000 miles to escape its death. The butterfly has no borders in its way, no papers to produce and no tolls to pay to stay where it is warmer. The butterfly's flight is a beautiful thing, nature itself. Why is my flight from the winter of my life filled with shame?

When I come across a container with the date of Jabu's naturalization, I am jolted out of my daydream. My hand shakes when I open the lid to find a pair of eyes sitting on a heap of other losses.

Jabu's eyes!

I reach for the eyes to burn them but cannot shake off the unease, cannot ignore the churning in my stomach. *What would Asha do?* a voice inside me screams. Asha wouldn't burn her friend's eyes. Asha would throw a middle finger up and march out of the plant. *But Asha is gone*, a pragmatic voice in my head cautions me. *Don't be stupid.*

I quickly glance at the other burners and the security camera before slipping the eyes into my pocket. I immediately take my timed bathroom break. In the toilet, I stash the eyes in my bra. Women in the old homeland would keep their coin purses in their bras to avoid pickpockets. No one ever thinks to search inside a woman's bra. My heart hammers in my chest throughout the rest of my shift. When I leave the plant, I do not exhale when I walk past armed security guards who can probably smell the fear on me. I've already lost one friend, I say to myself with resolve. I will not lose another. I avert my gaze as all burners do. The guards do not stop me. I'm still holding my breath when I reach my second job.

My night job drowns out the smell of smoke and fills it with the laughter of children. I'm a sarungano. I carry the stories of our people inside me and pass them to the children born here, children who don't have to go through the ceremony. I try to train their tongues to speak the old language. The language is mangled on their tongues. I hold the language classes and story times in the basement of an old building, clandestinely organized by concerned parents who are too afraid to claim their heritage in public.

"Tell us the story of how our people left the homeland!" one of the children says with his broken tongue. The children gather around me like bees who've been denied honey, bees who've lost their queen and don't remember how to fly back home, a hive in disarray.

"Yes, please, it's my favorite story!" another chimes in.

"Okay, okay, settle down, children, I will tell the story of our exodus," I say. I clear my throat dramatically, and the children laugh.

"There once was a beautiful homeland with evergreen forests, all-year-round summer, and the bluest lakes. Beautiful people walked its land, our people had music, food, and so much love to power an entire city. People and animals were not the only beings that walked the land. The homeland was full of spirits, both good and bad. One day the shavi, an evil spirit, gave birth to four children, the little shavis. The children's names were Disease, War, Poverty, and Corruption. The four little shavis were hungry, and nothing in their mother's house could satisfy them. So she let them out to scavenge for food. From that day, War, Disease, Poverty, and Corruption plagued the homeland. The forests burned, the lakes ran red with blood, and a storm cloud settled above the homeland."

"I wish I could lock up the four children and throw away the key," grumbled a little boy. "I hate shavis."

"Not all spirits are evil," I say, continuing the story. "Dlozi, an ancestral spirit, gathered all the surviving people and led them towards the Matopos Hills, where there was a giant rock as big as the power plant towers here."

"This is my favorite part!" a little girl squealed.

"The dlozi touched the rock, and it opened up," I say. "The survivors disappeared into the rock. When the rock opened up again, they were in a better world."

"That's how we ended up here," a little girl says. "This is the other side of that rock."

"Yes, that is correct," I say.

"How did the survivors know?" the girl presses.

"What do you mean?" I ask.

"How did the survivors know that the other side of the rock would be a better world?" she asks.

I think of Jabu's eyes inside my bra, so close to my chest. I don't have an answer for her.

When I get home, Jabu has thrown away all his paints and burned his canvases. I present him with the eyes. He shrinks away from me, refusing to take them.

"Have you lost your mind, Rasika?" Jabu says.

"I couldn't burn your eyes," I say. "I couldn't do it."

"Everyone has to give up something, okay," he says.

"What if Asha was right? What if we keep some things?" I say. "They have already taken so much. Don't we get to hold on to one thing?"

Jabu shakes his head.

"They are your eyes, Jabu," I say. "They belong to you."

"If you get caught, you will be deported," Jabu says. "I will not lose my only remaining friend over my stupid eyes. Take them back to the power plant and burn them! I don't want them."

"My ceremony is tomorrow," I say, my voice quivering. "I have a good guess that they are going to take my stories from me."

"Maybe we can do something to prepare," Jabu says desperately. "Maybe if you write down the stories—"

"What they take is always more twisted than anyone can guess, Jabu," I say. "If I write them down, they will probably take away my ability to read. So many people have tried to cheat the system, but it doesn't work. Before they take whatever they are going to take, I would like to give something freely without coercion. Please, do this for me."

Jabu removes his dark sunglasses and reluctantly takes his eyes back. I've never been so happy to see anything as I am to see Jabu's tears again.

My ceremony is on a Friday. Jabu accompanies me. We are both silent on the way to the ceremony. Jabu wears his sunglasses still and carries a cane. His sight is a secret we will both carry in silence. I know Jabu wants to tell me not to go through with the ceremony, but he cannot bring himself to say it. We have come too far to turn back now. Besides, what is there to turn back to? The only way is forward; people like us have nothing to go back to. For some reason I cannot get the little girl's question out of my mind. *How did the survivors know that the other side of the rock would be a better world?* I push away her voice. The little girl was born here, born a citizen. She doesn't understand what we sacrificed to be here.

Jabu and I sit outside the oath room like visitors outside a hospital room. One by one, freshly made citizens run out through the sliding doors, driven mad by what was taken from them. I think of the little shavis War, Disease, Poverty, and Corruption ravaging my homeland. *No price is too big,* I chant to myself like a prayer. *No price is too big to never see the shavis again.*

"Brother, what did they take from you?" Jabu asks a man who comes limping out. The man frowns in confusion. He doesn't understand us. I wonder, was it language that they took or his mind?

The young woman who comes out after him is in no better shape. All the blood has drained from her face. We don't even ask her what the priests took before she slumps to the floor next to us. She clutches my knees, trying to hold on to something, anything.

"They took my family," she says. "They took my entire family!"

I want to say something hopeful to her, to tell her she will be okay, to tell her that family separations are not uncommon, to tell that if she ignores the loneliness of citizenship, perhaps one day she won't even notice it, that we are all missing someone, that we have all lost someone, that is the nature of this side of the rock and if she works hard, she can do better and it will all have been worth it. The security guards drag her away from us before I can say any of that.

When it is my turn, I take a deep breath and enter the oath room. The naturalization priest assigned to me doesn't look at me, he looks past me as if I'm not even here, in the same way that those walking in the streets look past the homeless. The priest is dressed in a red robe, his collar decorated with stars to hold in place his pale, wraithlike face. He instructs me to put my hand to my heart for the oath of citizenship.

"Repeat after me," the priest says. "I renounce and abjure all allegiance and fidelity to any foreign sovereign or homeland of whom or of which I have heretofore been a citizen. I will support and defend my new homeland, I agree to bear arms on behalf of my new homeland, and I give my heart and soul to these lands."

The oath is a spell binding me to this land. My voice shakes, there is a tightness at the pit of my stomach. I should feel joy and relief. I'm finally becoming a citizen. Why don't I feel joy?

"I give my consent to pay the price the new homeland demands for the honor to be named a citizen," the priest incants.

"I give my consent to pay the price the new homeland demands for the honor to be named a citizen," I repeat. My voice is a whisper as I give the priest the proverbial blank cheque. I don't know what the new homeland will ask of me, will take from me. The priest lays a thumb on my forehead, his touch so gentle it could almost be a kiss.

"Congratulations," the priest says. "You are now a citizen."

When I blink, I am in a room, a priest is congratulating me.

"Rasika," another man behind me says. "What did they take from you? Did they take your stories?"

This man has on sunglasses, he holds a white cane in his right hand, and he speaks softly to me as if we've known each other for years.

"Who are you?" I ask.

The man doubles back as if I've slapped him.

"Rasika," he says again, desperation lacing every syllable he hits. "It's me—your friend—Jabu."

"I don't know who you are," I say. I pity him, I can see his face contorting into a full range of emotions—pain, rage, despair. Why is he so upset? I don't even know him.

"I hope you find who you are looking for," I say. "I am not Rasika."

"Remember, we're from—" The man who calls himself Jabu says the name of some place I've never heard of.

"I don't know where that is," I say. "You must be mistaken. I am a citizen of this land."

"If you are not Rasika, then tell me, what is your name?" this Jabu says.

I search my mind. I know the answer is at the tip of my tongue, but I cannot reach it.

"My name is . . . My name is—I am—I—I—" I stammer.

Come on, I know this, I scream at myself. I should know this. I have a name. It is right there, I can almost form the name on my lips, but it escapes me each time I get close to the answer.

"I don't know who I am," I say. A wave of nausea hits me.

The man who calls himself Jabu, calls himself my friend, crumples to the ground as if he cannot hold himself up anymore, as if his life is too much for his feet to bear. When he says my name again, the name I do not remember, his voice is an elegy.

The Carnivore's Lollipop

The ant box came with a set of instructions. Spritz the black garden ants with a solution of sugar and honey at dawn and again at dusk. Every three days, feed the ants steak—rare, the center juicy and pink like azaleas in full bloom. Treat the ants to snacks in between, such as cake, champagne, and dragon fruit. Under no circumstances open the lid.

It was easy work. Every forty days, I rode to the headquarters with my box and exchanged it for money. I didn't know what happened to the ants afterwards. I'd heard whispers that they were ground into some kind of powder. I didn't ask any questions, just got my cash.

Ignoring the water dripping from my ceiling, I fed the ants coconut cake through a slit in the box. The ants swarmed, demolishing it one slice at a time.

"Not even I eat this good," I sang to the little bastards. "But you eating good means I eat decent."

On my first day with the ant box, I remembered, I'd followed a YouTube recipe titled "The Carnivore's Lollipop." I rubbed the lamb chops with fresh thyme and marinated them in white wine, then seared them in a hot skillet with clarified butter and finished them with an apricot glaze. The little things had devoured the lamb chops in ten seconds—fat, meat, everything but the bone all gone.

After feeding the ants their cake, I lifted the box and headed out the door, ripping off the eviction notice tacked to my doorjamb before my approaching neighbor could notice it. My nasty landlady had raised the rent so high that ant breeding wasn't enough to keep this place anymore.

"I've been thinking about the ant breeding gig you told me about," my neighbor said as I quickly crumpled the notice into a ball. "Things have been tough this month. Need extra cash. You say it pays good?"

"Ant breeding has been keeping the lights on since the hyperinflation of 2008," I said. "Make sure to use my referral code. It can't hurt to try if the first time is free."

Outside, I loaded the box onto my bicycle and rode into town, the eviction notice rustling in my pocket.

"Thou shalt not steal" is a commandment that my gogo cauterized into my heart like a wound. When I was young, she would tell me ngano about all the bad things that happened to people who became tsotsis. One year my family were all kumusha for Christmas. My brothers, being city boys that rarely saw the countryside, had gone cow herding with the other boys as soon as dawn broke. As the cows passed by, the bells around their necks chiming in tune with the boys' laughter, I'd asked Gogo why cows had bells and why all the boys around here herded together. Wouldn't they get confused about which cow belonged to which household?

"They use the sound to track when the cows are out of view, mwana wemwana wangu," Gogo said. "And everyone knows which cow belongs to who."

"What about thieves? If they allow the cows to just roam around, someone might steal them!" I'd exclaimed.

"No one steals around here," Gogo said with an unnerving confidence.

She told me about a city boy who'd come back kumusha, stolen a cow, and sold it in another village. Before he'd even finished counting the money, his stomach growled. The sound, of course, wouldn't have turned heads if it had not been a moo. From that day, everywhere he went, his stomach mooed as if he'd eaten a kraal full of harmonizing cattle.

"That is why nobody here steals," Gogo said. "They know better."

"What happened to the boy?" I asked, horrified, my hand resting protectively over my belly.

"He had to come back, find the owner of the cow he'd stolen, and ripa," Gogo said.

At my confused expression, Gogo explained that kuripa was paying what is owed for damages done. Reparations.

Usually there would be a long line outside headquarters as breeders dropped off their boxes one by one like little ants marching towards a colony. But today the single-file symmetry had devolved into a frenzied crowd carrying placards and chanting the slogans hastily scribbled on cardboard.

> VUKA VUKA MUST FALL!
> WHERE IS OUR MONEY?
> PASI NE MBAVHA!
> PANSI NGAMASELA!

I hopped off my bicycle but didn't make it far. Police were blocking the entrance.

"The CEO dissolved the company," another ant breeder said to me as we locked eyes. "I spent a fortune buying organic dragon fruit for my ants. How will I get my money back?"

The box shook in my hands. I had to sell the ants.

The day grew darker and angrier. I did not move as others holding ant boxes tossed petrol bombs into the building, jumped on top of parked cars and lit them on fire. Police in riot gear bludgeoned anyone within reach. I stood frozen in the midst of it all, hoping that soon the doors of the burning building would somehow open, my check for the month waiting inside.

One breeder wrenched open her box and hurled it at an officer. The ants clumped around him as if he were a piece of shrimp, his blue and gray uniform swarming with a mass of black. When the ants were done, only bones and the uniform remained. Soon other breeders did the same with their boxes.

The riot police retreated from the onslaught, the ants chasing after them—an army of tiny soldiers turning the streets into a black river. I clutched my box tighter.

The remaining police officers shot live bullets at the crowd, driving the demonstrators back. Three officers tackled an elderly ant breeder to the ground, twisting her hands behind her. Suddenly a cloud of tear gas mushroomed around my feet. My eyes burned, and a weight settled into my chest. I broke into a blind run, the old woman's harrowed screams ringing in my ears.

There is a ngano about a rich landlady that Gogo used to tell around the fire. This woman owned one of those big high-rise flats, kuma avenues, that looked like bricks against the sky. She was known for kicking out families without notice, bullying her tenants with her two drunkard sons, and withholding deposits without explanation. She also sat front row at church every Sunday. One Sunday, while carrying her brown Louis Vuitton bag after a nice service about how there is no place for avarice in the Kingdom of God to which she had yelled amen, she saw a hive dangling from a tree in the parking lot. Before she could unlock her Rolls-Royce Phantom, the hive burst like fireworks, unleashing a thousand angry bees. Each sting radiated across her body like a whip, and she swore she could see the faces of everyone she'd ever wronged on their hairy heads. She removed all her clothing, threw her Louis Vuitton bag on the ground, and ran, leaving her car behind. The bees swarmed the bag.

Pouring milk over the eyes relieves the sting of tear gas, but in this city, milk is a unicorn. With the twelve-hour power cuts, supermarkets don't carry fresh milk anymore, just powdered in tin cans. I couldn't find my bicycle. I cursed whoever had stolen it. My eyes itched as I limped home, the ant box heavier than before. The bicycle would find its way back to me eventually.

When I got home, I fed the ants and turned on the news while I heated up my dinner of sadza and boiled beans. I half-listened to the news anchor dish out the week's misfortunes as I ate, until she mentioned the headquarters.

"Vuka Incorporated was the manufacturer of a popular over-the-counter drug called Vuka Vuka, also known as Rise Rise, a Viagra-like pill which saw billions in sales last year. A whistleblower revealed the drug's formula."

Footage of pill bottles dissolved into a close-up of ants rushing out of an anthill. The camera settled on two pundits in the studio.

"This is the biggest Ponzi scheme of the decade," one suited man said. "Millions of low-skilled and unemployed people were duped into ant breeding by subscribing to a fifteen-hundred-dollar-a-month ant box scheme."

Footage of the protest played as the pundit spoke. My heart clenched as the camera focused on me for a moment in the crowd. Had my braids always been so tousled, my eyes so empty? I was just standing there hugging the ant box while others raged around me. The camera panned to burning cars.

"These breeders exchanged the ant boxes for seventeen hundred dollars. That's a profit margin of a mere two hundred dollars, and most of that money went into taking care of the ants with expensive food . . . "

Once, while Gogo crushed groundnuts with her mortar and pestle, she told me about a land dispute. Two men both claimed hectares of fertile land as their family's ancestral land. Neither of them had a title deed to prove ownership, for what is a piece of paper to memory? They hurled insults at each other and exchanged blows before bringing their dispute before a dare. I was fascinated as Gogo explained to me how the traditional Shona court system worked, how it was presided over not by judges or lawyers but by a chief, just like in the old days. The chief was presented with the facts as the two aggrieved parties saw them. He said he would consult an advisor before making a decision.

The chief travelled to the city, making a stop at ZINATHA's headquarters, an unassuming building in the middle of the central business district. The Zimbabwe Traditional Healers Association offices looked much like a therapist's office except that instead of a couch and white noise machines, there were mats, bones, calabashes, and cowrie shells. The chief explained the case to Arumando, an old sangoma, who gave him two chickens.

"How will chickens help me judge this case?" the chief asked.

"From a court composed of chickens, can corn ever expect justice?" the sangoma said, and offered no more.

The chief mulled over the sangoma's words on his way back to dare, and was no closer to making a decision about how to handle the case. In the morning, when the two men returned to hear the chief's decision about which of them would get the land, the chief cracked his knuckles nervously, for he had not come to a decision that seemed fair and just. He stared at the two chickens he'd been given, and suddenly an idea popped into his head.

"You will each bury a chicken tonight," the chief said. "Then come back tomorrow to dig it up, cook it, and eat it right here in front of the dare. Only the chicken buried by the rightful owner of this land will be accepted as an offering by the ancestors. The other chicken will turn into poison. Whoever dies from taking a bite is the liar and never had a right over the land."

One of the men shook with such fright that he dropped both the shovel and the chicken he'd been given and ran for the hills. The one who stayed was given the land.

Gogo's nganos kept me up at night when ZESA would go and the house was consumed by darkness. Her favorite was of a politician who pocketed donor money meant to provide piped water to his constituency. He bought a mansion and two cars and put his children through top private schools. One day he was outside, watching the sprinkler's spray nourish his ever-green lawn as a garden boy trimmed the hedges, when a left hook landed on his jaw. Reeling back, he thought at first that the garden boy had struck him, but the garden boy was too far away to have done it. The politician looked around frantically and saw no one. Before he had time to process this, a kick to the groin and a bitch slap to the face sent him to his knees. After a week of taking blows he couldn't see, his black cheeks were swollen and deep purple like African violets. Gogo called it a chidhoma attack. The invisible goblins controlled by varoyi only stopped beating him up after he went to every household in his constituency and paid them the damages owed.

When I was eight, a boy stole my bicycle. That night, I called Gogo crying, and she told me to wipe my tears because no one steals from us. While we were on the phone, the boy rode home. As soon as he got off, the bicycle spoke:

"Ndidzosere kumba kwawakanditora."

Return me from whence I came.

A migraine throbbed at my temples as I ignored my neighbor angrily banging on the door. I thought back to a Facebook friend who'd invited me to ant breed through a post—*want to make money and set your own hours?* Soon after that, I was convincing others to breed ants too. I received a bonus every month for every person who signed up with my referral code, and then another bonus when they got another person to sign up.

"The CEO Edgar Vuka sponsored lobby groups to get the Traditional Medicines Act passed," the news anchor reported, "which made it legal for pharmacies across the country to sell this untested drug."

Edgar Vuka's mansion in Borrowdale Brooke and his garage full of imported cars filled the screen alongside photographs of him with the president receiving an Entrepreneur of the Year Award. If corn cannot expect justice in a court composed of chickens, what then must the corn do?

I switched off the TV, wondering how many others I had led into financial ruin. I knew I must ripa. I lifted the lid of the ant box and peered inside. The ants were a terrifying undulating glob, ready to charge.

I slammed the lid shut and latched it, thinking of all the ngano that Gogo had ever told me. As I walked into the night, the box on my shoulder, I knew I wasn't the only one marching in single file towards Borrowdale Brooke. We would give the ants a meal that was even richer than before.

Swimming with Crocodiles

My grandmother sang to a streetlamp, her arms outstretched as if willing its broken light to come into her bosom. Gogo always sang the war songs, the ones she and other comrades sang at Chimoio camp right before the Rhodesian planes dropped their fire and took her left eye. The people in the growing queue checked their watches and stared as she moved away from the lamp to serenade a parked car.

"Nyika yedu yeZimbabwe," Gogo sang. "Beautiful beautiful Zimbabwe."

The line for Barclays Bank stretched from its closed doors to the Total petrol station downtown. It snaked past the now-defunct Kingdom Bank and the never-ending rows of street vendors. I kept an eye out for Gogo as I balanced a box of bananas on my head, trying to catch the queuers' eyes. Bananas sold the quickest these days. I suppressed a groan when Gogo repeated the word "beautiful." Perhaps she couldn't see the queues through her one eye.

To test the presence of starch in food, use iodine solution, a dropper, and a white tile.

I repeated to myself the experiment I'd read in Zuva's study notes as Gogo sang. Some people in the queue wiped away the sleep from their eyes, stretched, and packed up old newspapers or zambiyas into their bags. They'd slept outside the bank for a chance to be in the lucky first three hundred to be allowed to withdraw their money.

I looked over at Gogo to make sure she didn't stray too far down the road. I tried to compare her to the pictures I'd seen of her before she lost her eye, when she was just beginning as a soldier. Hands steady on a gun. Two seeing eyes leveled at the camera. I couldn't find the woman in the photograph in the woman in front of me.

To test the presence of starch in food, use iodine solution, a dropper, and a white tile.

"Nyika yemavendor, gogo," a young man said, fed up with Gogo's singing.

The young man's comment about how we were now a country of vendors—everyone selling something, with only a lucky few with the cash to buy—only fueled Gogo's patriotic fervor.

"Simudza gumbo," she sang as she mimicked the goose step. "Hai, hai, hai."

People broke into laughter. Gogo, the daily entertainment. The regulars had come to call her Comrade Gogo Blaze. Blaze was the nom de guerre she took up during the war.

"She thinks we are still kuhondo," a woman said, flicking her tightly twisted braids. "The war is long over, ambuya."

The middle-aged man behind her belched out a laugh, not because his belly was full but because one can only laugh when there is nothing to smile about. He seemed to pass the laughter down to the woman behind him until it spread to the rest of the queue like dominos. "Comrade Blaze is doing the simudza gumbo again."

When Gogo wasn't singing war songs, she told me war stories.

"War is not easy, mwana wemwana wangu," she said every night before she lay down on the bonde. The old straw mat did not cushion us from the hard floor. We shared our home, a one-bedroom in Nkulumane, with two other families. "Pray you never see what I've seen."

Even though I'd heard the story before, I still gave her my full attention.

"I was at a mission boarding school when the soldiers came to the girls' dorms one night. They marched us out in our nightdresses and said we were now freedom fighters," she began, her voice far away in another time. "We forgot books and learned about the gun. But it wasn't only the gun we had to learn. We had to learn other things . . ." Her voice trailed off. "We not only fought but we cooked, we washed the soldiers' uniforms, we . . . we . . . The generals and soldiers needed services only women could provide." Then she would turn and close her eyes, each night fighting off someone in her sleep. I could not tell if it was a Rhodesian or another freedom fighter.

1. *Put a slice of each food being tested on the white tile.*
2. *Using a dropper, add drops of iodine solution to each food.*
3. *Wait for a few minutes and observe the color changes on each foodstuff.*

The morning traffic picked up. The bananas were already sold. I laid out a newspaper on the pavement, holding it in place against the wind using four granite rocks. I wondered what it was like to be inside a science lab at school, holding a dropper or a beaker and discovering something new. I placed packets of Jiggies and salted maputi on top of the newspapers. A group of schoolchildren passed without glancing at me.

It was a welcome relief that I now came here late at night or in the early morning to set up as people trickled in to line up for the bank. Losing sleep was better than hearing Gogo's nightmares. Anyway, coming here early had become very profitable. The queuers were hungry, tired, and frustrated. Frustrated people made the best customers.

Tired of standing in line, a man in blue overalls bought some Jiggies with his last dollar and went to sit by the curb.

"I have been here the whole week and I still can't withdraw any money," he said. He wasn't talking to anyone in particular. People in the line grumbled in sympathy. Zuva, a friend I'd gone to primary school with, smiled and waved at me from her spot in the line. Her mother beside her regarded me with a disapproving eye.

"Look at it, dead and empty," the man in overalls said. He pointed at a line of rusting ATMs outside the bank. They hadn't been used in a year.

"All we can do is leave it up to Jesu," a woman said. She was wearing the black and red Methodist Church uniform. "Only God knows."

I had become a street vendor five years ago when the school accountant rounded up everyone in grade seven who had not paid their school fees and sent them home. Gogo marched us, in the cap she wore when she was a freedom fighter, to the War Veterans Association and demanded to see whoever was in charge.

"I am a war vet," she said to the pretty secretary who looked no older than twenty. "My grandchild shouldn't have to suffer."

"I'm sorry, the chairman is not taking any appointments this week," the secretary said, not looking up from the computer. "The Association doesn't handle payment of school fees."

"The *chwemen*, the *chwemen*," Gogo said mimicking the secretary's twang. "That mafikizolo isn't even a war vet. I fought for this country. The reason you can sit your fat buttocks on that chair today is because I—"

Gogo was interrupted by the security guard's rough hands and we were yanked out of the offices. Gogo's cap fell to the ground during the scuffle. She never retrieved it.

With no money for fees, I started standing outside my school every day, hands curled against the fence. I watched students walking in the corridors, playing on the playground, and eating lunch. Zuva would sneak outside the school through a hole in the fence during break time to see me.

"We've started preparing for the high school entrance exams," Zuva said, handing me a pile of her exercise books. I grabbed them and ravenously scanned the pages, taking in everything I saw, asking her what each assignment meant.

"Can I have your math textbook this weekend?" I asked, leafing through it, yearning for the problem sets, yearning for the luxury of detesting math like Zuva.

"Sure, I wasn't going to study anyway," Zuva said. My education over the years consisted of reading Zuva's notes and books, asking her to explain concepts I didn't quite grasp.

Zuva pulled out a lunchbox from her bag. I averted my eyes. "Have you eaten today?" she asked. I shook my head.

Zuva had three sandwiches. She broke one in half and ate it.

"I don't like polony but my mom keeps packing it," she said, pushing the lunchbox with the rest of her sandwiches into my hands. "You can have the rest."

I refused her food even though my stomach complained. Being pitied was worse than hunger.

Observation: iodine turns blue-black when it comes in contact with starch.

Barclays Bank was located opposite Bulawayo Center, the two-story mall in Bulawayo's central business district that no one frequented. Barclays was supposed to open its doors at 8 a.m. At 9 a.m. the young man who had made remarks earlier about Gogo's singing let out a sonorous *nxa*, sucking in his teeth to sum up his anger. The gleaming glass doors remained closed.

"We will wait here until we get into our graves," the young man said, punctuating his words with another *nxa* and removing his bucket hat to reveal short locks that coiled like bean sprouts. "Watch. Even after waiting in line for so long, we will only be allowed to withdraw fifty dollars."

"Right now I am missing work to line up here to get last month's pay," the man in overalls responded. "But what else can I do?" No one had an answer for him.

A woman, her thin body weighed down by a heavy pregnancy, was dropped off in front of the bank by a kombi that nearly ran over those sitting by the curb as it reversed back into the street. Some men in the line mumbled insults under their breath. Pregnant women, the handicapped, and elderly people automatically went to the front of the line.

"We came here to queue at three a.m. and you just come now and go to the front," one man shouted at the woman. "Lying on your back pays off."

"Can't you see she is pregnant?" the Methodist woman chided.

A bearded old man standing behind a woman carrying a baby on her back was making smiley faces at the baby, who laughed and cooed in response. The old man stuck his tongue out, scratched his beard, and rolled his eyes like they were about to pop out of their sockets. Some schoolboys in their uniforms walked past. I thought about Zuva. She was taking her ZIMSEC O-Level exams in two weeks. I still needed some more biology notes from her.

"Have you heard the rumors?" said a smartly dressed young woman. "They are bringing back Zim dollar."

I left the chips and sweets laid out on the pavement and walked down the queue peddling my cooler box full of Cascade juices and freeze-its. My grandmother didn't know I had a jar of money stashed away. From each sale, I kept 40 cents. If I kept it up, I could have enough to register for the O-Level exams. I hadn't been in school since I was twelve, yet I wanted to take the most important national exams.

"No," the queue said in unison. For the first time that morning, a hush fell on the queue.

"My cousin has a friend whose brother works at the Reserve Bank in Harare, and he said there is a new currency coming," she insisted. "That's why there are all these withdrawal limits. They are stealing our US dollars and swapping them for this new currency!"

"I've heard these rumors, too," another person said. "I heard they are going to be called bond notes."

"It will be 2008 all over again. It's already started with the return of these queues. My grandson who works at the Passport Office says they don't even have paper to print out new passports. Passports have been backlogged since last year."

"I have a master's degree. This shouldn't be my life," someone said.

"Who doesn't have a degree in this line?" the young man with locs said. "Yet I'm a malaicha."

Malaichas were cross-border drivers who were known to smuggle all sorts of things, like groceries and people.

"With these passport backlogs, might as well get a malaicha to help me border-jump eBeitbridge like everyone else," someone else said.

Since 2008, talking about the best way to border-jump was just as commonplace as asking for restaurant recommendations.

"You will be eaten by crocodiles!" Gogo exclaimed.

The border between Zimbabwe and South Africa at Beitbridge stretches along the crocodile-infested Limpopo River. In 2008, when the price of bread rose from ZIM$5 billion to ZIM$15 billion, and then to a trillion, many young men and women decided that swimming with crocodiles was better than living on dry land.

"What's the difference, masalu?" said the malaicha. "Why should I care about the crocodiles in the Limpopo when there is a crocodile in the State House?"

"All you young people today, all you know how to do is run away," Gogo said, spitting on the ground near the young man's shoes and pointing a dirty fingernail at everyone in the line. "In my day, we didn't run away from our problems. We took up pfuti and fought for our freedom. Zimbabwe will never be a colony again!"

"Matakadya kare hanyaradzi mwana," he said. "Your war songs are not going to feed us. What has your hondo done for you, really? You lost your eye just to sell tomatoes in the streets!"

My grandmother raised her walking stick as she shuffled towards the young man. The imminent fight was defused by the bank's doors slowly squeaking open.

Cohesion is the force whereby individual molecules stick together. Adhesion is the force whereby water molecules stick to other surfaces.

A security guard dressed in a freshly ironed Safeguard uniform walked out with a stack of forms, the forms people needed to withdraw their money. The guard walked at his leisure with his chest pushed out like a cockerel. He made a show of counting the forms. There were fifty of them, as always. A hush fell over the queue as they watched the white pieces of paper being shuffled in the guard's hands. They were like newborns waiting for the nipple.

"Salibonani abantu abahle," he greeted us without cheer. He put a finger on his tongue to collect some spit to help him pick the papers apart. He looked up and scanned the crowd like he was Jesus about to distribute loaves and fishes. The crowd gaped back eagerly at him, hoping to catch his eye.

"Come on, we don't have all day," a man exclaimed. He was so thin, his shirt looked like it was a dress.

"Get out of the line," the guard said sternly. "Go on, go home! You are not ready to have your money today." The guard shooed the man away like a stray dog.

"Anyone else with anything to say?" he challenged the crowd. Some shook their heads, some looked down. Others continued to smile to catch the guard's eye. The guard counted off fifty people from the line. The elderly, disabled, and pregnant women were usually the ones most likely to be picked. Then strong-looking men, pretty light-skinned women, and people that knew the guard personally.

"Sorry, but the rest of you have to go home. We don't have enough forms," the guard said, clearing his throat after he had given away the last form. "Those of you with forms, please count off in groups of ten. Only ten people can go inside at a time."

The unchosen groaned and began to move away, among them the man in blue overalls. A few rushed up to the guard, cracking a joke with him and asking him about his family. They hoped that the guard would remember them next time. Some stayed and formed a new line for tomorrow.

"Would you ever border-jump?" I asked Zuva. She was in her high school's uniform. Her mother shuffled towards the bank, leaving her behind.

"I can't even swim, mgane," she responded, as the guard called out one last instruction. I doubted that the restless malaicha with the bean-sprout locs could swim, either.

"At least my mother managed to get in today, so we can finally pay my exam fees," Zuva said. "I think wearing my school uniform made the guard pick us."

"Please be considerate of others. No pushing, no shoving, please!" the guard shouted over the rush of feet. "No mawalas, or I will send you home!"

"I hope things work out for you, mgane," Zuva said. She waited until her mother had disappeared inside before reaching into her pocket. "Here."

"I think you should save the money for a rainy day," I said, shaking my head.

"I'll be fine," she said, placing some dollars in my hands. "Hope to see you again at school one day, mgane." Zuva squeezed my hand and went to wait by the door of the bank.

"Hey, wena. I want to buy a frozeni," said the restless malaicha who had gotten into an argument with my grandmother. He approached me. He was among the chosen.

It always amazed me how one thing could go by so many names. Some called the ice pops I sold freeze-its, others frozens, and others supercools. It was said that only rich people who went to private schools with white people called them supercools.

"What color do you want?" I asked, inching the cooler box closer to his face.

"Red," he said as he dug into his back pocket for some money. "The color of love."

I resisted the urge to roll my eyes. I'd learned long ago to let the men flirt. The longer they talked, the more they bought and the fuller my jar got.

"Also the color of blood," I said, keeping an eye on Gogo, who was standing at attention, reciting the names of all the soldiers who lost their lives at Chimoio.

"What's your name, s'thandwa?" he asked. The word "m'love" rolled off his tongue. He said it the way all men say it, with their eyes peeling my skin apart like fruit.

"Hondo," I said, handing him a frozen packet and pocketing the money.

The young man stared at me for a count of ten. I could tell he wasn't sure whether I was serious or not. He opened his mouth to speak and then closed it again.

"Your name is Hondo? War?" he finally said. "You are not serious?"

"Are you going to buy anything else?" I asked. "Some Jiggies would go well with that."

"I'm Sibusiso," he said, handing me more money. "Who named you?"

"My grandmother," I said, looking in her direction.

The young man gave me a knowing nod of condolence. It didn't need to be said; he could tell instantly what had taken my parents.

"I guess your gogo loved the war so much that she wanted to be reminded of it each time she called your name," he said, opening his freeze-it with his teeth, the red juice trickling down his lips. "Some people just won't stop living in the past."

He sucked on the freeze-it until it lost its color.

"Listen, if you ever get tired of selling Jiggies," he said, and handed me his phone number. "A fine girl like you belongs in South Africa. I can make it happen."

Gogo was running down the pavement, holding her walking stick up like a gun. She made the sound of gunfire and explosions. I still had a lot more to save up until I made enough money to pay for the O-Level exams. I considered the malaicha's proposal as he moved forward along with his group of ten, making a beeline for the bank's open doors. Looking at the streetlamps around me, I wondered who would fix the broken lights.

Ugly Hamsters: A Triptych

God Will Provide

Gods work at the Bank of America financial center. Perched on the corner of Pleasant Street in Amherst, Massachusetts, it looks to the naked eye like any other bank outfitted with ATMs, tellers, and plexiglass counters. Imali stands outside the large doors with a pink Steve Madden suitcase, dark sunglasses, and red bottom heels. She tucks a strand of her silk press behind her ear, her mouth set in a grim line. This is her punishment for unplugging the prayer hotline, thereby not meeting her monthly quota of prayers. The bastard upstairs relocated her from the New York branch to this middle-of-bumfuck-nowhere town. Small-town humans are her least favorite mortals. She is to report to her desk by 9 a.m., but haste isn't something an immortal is familiar with, so she lights a Marlboro and takes a detour to the bakery down the street.

Prayer-granting duties are the worst drudgery of being a goddess, right up there with number crunching and managing family fortune accounts. She would even take filling out birth and death spreadsheets, like Papa Legba who sits in the cubicle next to her, over listening to whiny, desperate prayers. Being a goddess of wealth, she gets a lot of them from entitled businessmen who screw people over with one hand while begging the gods for favor with the other. But a certain number of prayers must be granted so people can continue to believe in the divine. Most prayers are usually about money or would be solved by money, so Imali's hotline is always busy, second only to the god of love, but even the god of love sometimes forwards some prayers to her because human intimacy is so transactional.

But I'm not the Creator, so who am I to question the Creator's design? she thinks as she enters the little bakery and orders coconut cake. *That is above my pay grade. That damn bastard. Gods should unionize.*

She sprinkles a pinch of prosperity in the air before she leaves. She quite likes the way they make coconut cake so fluffy here and doesn't want this business to close down. Outside, her mood is immediately ruined by the sudden reek of financial stress in the air. While rich people leave a sickly sweet fragrance wherever they go, those who are not so blessed have a pungent odor. The smell curdles the coconut in her stomach. She has to know the source of foulness and correct it immediately. She sniffs and chokes back her bile as the odor grows overwhelmingly strong. Her eyes rest on a young woman walking on the opposite side of the street. Her shoulders are hunched, her brow creased with worry, and she clutches her purse as if it is a heartbeat she is trying to resuscitate. A Zimbabwean student attending one of the five colleges in the area on a need-based scholarship. Imali crosses the road and follows the Zimbabwean girl all the way to the Western Union. Sending money she doesn't even have to her struggling family back home. Money she makes working late shifts at the campus dining hall at the expense of her grades. This isn't the first time Imali's seen the bubonic plague of wealth, black tax, at work. Imali waits outside and watches through the window as the girl hands off every last cent to the Western Union agent. The girl will probably be back here again next month performing the same endless ritual of poverty. The girl has on a T-shirt with GOD WILL PROVIDE in bold lettering. *Your faith is misplaced,* girl, Imali thinks. As if on cue, the girl wrings her hands and prays under her breath. What she prays for surprises Imali. The girl doesn't pray for more money, which would be the sensible thing to do. The girl prays for a day off.

I'm not on the clock yet; I should just walk away, Imali thinks, crossing her arms. But something gnaws at the goddess of wealth. It isn't often she feels anything other than indifference to a human—they are no more than the Creator's ugly pet hamsters running in place—but Imali sees something of herself in the girl. Both subject to a system created by those more powerful.

I deserve a fucking raise for this overtime, she thinks. But Imali knows the Creator isn't generous and doesn't reward gods and goddesses who go beyond the minimum expected of them to keep the universe in motion. Imali takes a crisp five-dollar bill from her wallet, kisses it, and places it at the door of the Western Union just as the Zimbabwean girl is stepping out.

Black Tax

Light is still feeling that black hole of emptiness, which soon hardens into resentment at giving out of necessity, when she sees Abraham Lincoln's grim face staring up at her. She is trying not to think about the money she's just sent home for her brother's school fees, her gogo's hospital bill, and her mama's rent. The five-dollar bill is crisp and clean, like it's just come out of an ATM. She looks up and down the street but doesn't see anyone who appears to have dropped their money. She pauses for a moment, deciding whether or not to pick it up. Mama taught her from a young age never to pick up money whose origins she didn't know. Mama believes that witches leave money on sidewalks to lure people into blood money cults. Once you pick up the money, you are automatically inducted. But this is America, Light chides herself. There is no magic here. Light thinks of her gogo, who has a slightly different philosophy from Mama's. Gogo believes that walking away from found money is an insult to the goddess of wealth, and if you slight the goddess of wealth, she will never bless you again. Gogo also believes that just in case the money isn't a gift from Imali but a cursed bill from a blood cult, all you have to do is step on the money a bunch of times to stomp the curse out of the cash. Light lifts her foot, ready to crash the bill under her well-worn shoes, but she stops herself. How ridiculous she would look in this white town, stepping on money like a madwoman. She would be too embarrassed to hand a bill with a dirty shoe print on it to a cashier. She snatches up the money instead, quickly stashes it in her purse, and heads to the bus stop wondering if she has invited misfortune into her life.

Light can't afford a meal plan, because she is using the part of her scholarship meant for her meals to send money back home. The on-campus pantry for food-insecure students is the only reason she doesn't starve. With only the five dollars in her pocket, she walks into the campus cafe and buys a breakfast bagel for $4.75. The disinterested student cashier smacking gum between his lips gives her ten dollars as change.

"You gave me too much change," Light says.

The cashier blinks at Light like she is stupid. "Your change is ten bucks," the cashier says, rolling his eyes before he shouts, "Next in line!"

Light quickly moves off, feeling the ten-dollar bill's weight before she stuffs it into her pocket. She is confused by her luck today and decides to get a drink from the vending machine. The machine spits out twenty dollars in change. Something is afoot here, she thinks. She buys one more thing just to make sure she isn't going crazy and gets two hundred in change. She decides to test it further by going to the campus store to buy the expensive textbook needed for her linguistics course that the professor doesn't bother to put on reserve at the library because professors assume everyone has two hundred to drop per book. She walks away with a thousand in change. She goes on a shopping spree at the mall, buying herself all the things she's ever wanted. Sturdy winter boots, a coat that actually keeps out the cold, a laptop so she doesn't have to rent one from the Office of Equity and Inclusion. She can't wait to get to the library and write an essay on a device that's hers only. By the end of the day, she is thousands of dollars richer. When she returns to her dorm room, she lines the floor with hundred-dollar bills. Light lies down and sweeps her arms and legs on top of the money like snow angels. What should I do with the money next? She books a spa session.

In the middle of a hot stone massage, the massage therapist tells her she carries a lot of tension in her shoulders and could she relax a little? That one word is a thread unraveling. Light is undone. Guilt settles in. How could she be enjoying a spa treatment in America when her family back home could use the money? Another word takes root in her mind, its spores spreading through her veins. Selfish, selfish, selfish. She bolts from the treatment table, the massage therapist begging her to lie down because they aren't done yet, but Light cannot hear anything but her guilt. She runs back to the Western Union, mentally listing everything her family needs. Funeral costs for her uncle who passed on because he couldn't afford the lifesaving medication for his condition, school fees for the three children he left behind. Passport fees, including the bribe to make the government officials process them faster, for thirteen cousins looking to go to South Africa for greener pastures. From then onwards, every cent she receives, she sends home. Maternity fees for a shunned cousin who is fifteen and pregnant. Electricity installation in her gogo's rural home. Groceries, water bills, and

and

and

and

She gives and gives and gives and the list keeps growing, like putting out a fire for another to mushroom in its place. Every dollar that multiplies comes earmarked for some problem, until there is no room in her life for anything but the list. She wonders if she should have stepped on that five-dollar bill that day.

Ngano

Long long ago, before the earth was smashed by a hammer and life emerged from the cracks

Paivapo
There once was
Paivapo
There once was
Paivapo
There still is
the twin gods, Gamab and Gaunab, known collectively as the Creator, for they are conjoined at the neck. They built a village called heaven. Every second that passes, Gaunab brings his hammer down and creates life while Gamab shoot his celestial arrow of lightning to take it away. They watch a girl named Light driven mad by the goddess of wealth's favor. This is why they frown upon overtime: it throws things out of balance.

"I should put her out of her misery," Gamab says. He lifts his bow and pierces her body with his arrow.

Light's soul leaves her body, departing through the open window in her dorm room. Her body will be discovered in a week, and an email will be sent with the subject line "A Sad Loss to Our Community." People will whisper about stress, first generation, suic—

And then she will be forgotten.

But today is not yet that day. Today her soul takes the road that leads to Gamab and Gaunab's village. Light's soul remembers her mama's words that were a balm during the hard times. *You will be rewarded in heaven, where there is abundance.* Gamab and Gaunab sit by a fire telling stories about the beginning of time—"Paivapo," they call out—to the ancestors, who holler back, "Dzepfunde."

"Why?" she screams at the Creator. So many accusations hiss on her tongue. Why do you let black tax continue to plague us? Why can't we create generational wealth? I had so much potential—why couldn't I do it? Why didn't you answer my prayers? Light's soul is red and blue with fury that melts into sadness.

"Tell me, Light, have you heard the song 'Ancestors Working Full Time'?" the Creator says before singing the song they sing to every newly arrived soul, their two voices overlaid on top of each other. The song has an upbeat tempo that almost masks the hell in the lyrics. Before the song is over, she looks up. Light did not notice the large factory in the clouds at first, smoke billowing out of its chimneys.

"You can rest here, take your place amongst the ancestors around the fire, or you can work full time in the factory generating fortune for your living family," the Creator says after finishing the song. "Those are your two choices."

The Creator leads her to the factory. Inside, there are millions—no, billions—of human-sized hamster wheels with ancestors running in place.

"You've had a hard life, Light. You've always been the good oldest daughter," the Creator says. "No one will judge you for choosing rest."

When the ancestors run, they generate points on a little screen in front of them which, like wire transfers, are sent to Imali, who then calculates how much to credit to each family's account. Fortune trickles down the bloodline.

"Rest or the factory, Light?" the Creator asks, opening the little gate to the ancestral wheel.

Light makes her choice, lifting her foot towards her eternity.

Ndipo pakazoperera sarungano. This is where the storyteller ends.

Plumtree: True Stories

Ants

An hour had not yet passed, since Tanaka slept with his neighbor's wife, when ants squirted out of his manhood. Each time he felt the urge to piss, one by one little black ants crawled out from his shaft instead of a spray of urine. They did not come quietly, these ants. They bit into his flesh, tickled his veins with their antennae, and danced their way out of him with each of their six little legs.

Tanaka had made it a habit to sleep with other men's wives. He liked the power that came with releasing himself in someone who belonged to someone else. How was Tanaka to know that this woman in particular, Kurai's wife, was fixed?

He begged the elders for an answer.

The elders who smoked long pipes, sniffed tobacco, basked in the sun, and spoke of things unknown to the younger generation called it kugadzira mukadzi—to fix your wife. They said the words in hushed tones and laughed at Tanaka in between coughs and blowing smoke rings. They too had once cast spells on their wives. It was what you did when you married a beautiful woman. If any man but you tasted your wife's sweetness, that intruder would receive a nasty surprise on his way out.

The elders told another story of a man in a faraway town who took another man's wife from behind. He never came out. They went everywhere stuck together like that, the woman crawling on all fours with the man above her. Not even the country's top surgeon, who had successfully separated conjoined twins earlier that year, could separate the man and the woman.

Basket Women

I.

The Wright Brothers were not the first to find flight. There are other histories, other sciences not recorded, but in this world when something is not written down, it does not exist. Varoyi have known how to soar since before men learned to walk upright. Varoyi, those naked women in the forest with access to knowledge from the other side, lift off into the night from inside winnowing baskets. What men cannot do or understand is evil. So these naked women have been blamed for sickness and death, and their craft dismissed as witchery, not science.

II.

Gusheshe, a comedian from a small town in Zimbabwe, rose to national fame with her skits. As more and more people subscribed to her YouTube channel, her jokes became more daring. High on the euphoria of a million views, she imagined she could be like her South African hero Trevor Noah. Envisioning herself hosting a *Late Night* or a *Daily Show* in America, she mocked the government. The videos were liked and shared and liked and shared. This small-town girl's name travelled from lips to lips until it found itself in a Kill Folder.

The gunmen were swift breaking into her house, blindfolding her, and shoving her into the back of an Isuzu. Neighbors saw the whole thing, but who can call the police when the gunmen are the police? After hours of driving, they dropped Gusheshe blindfolded into sewage water.

"So you think you're funny?" one of the gunmen screamed at her. He kicked her in the stomach. They stuck her head under the water.

"Since you think you're funny," another gunman said, "make us laugh."

She heard six voices in total. Someone kicked her again with a boot. She knew that police wore red boots and soldiers wore black boots. She couldn't tell the color of the boots from the way they crushed against her skull.

"I said make us laugh," a gunman said.

They forced her mouth open and stuck her head under the water again. She tasted shit in her mouth. Her eyes watered. She retched and was shoved under again.

"A big-mouthed bitch like you can't swallow?" another said. "Gurgle the water in your mouth like you are brushing your teeth for a Colgate advert."

They laughed at their own jokes. Torture demands a certain kind of inventiveness; cruelty can turn a jailer into a comedian.

"Do you know why you are here?" a gunman said.

"Imagination is my only crime," Gusheshe replied after swallowing a mouthful of the water. This made the men angry. They kicked and punched her harder. Seeing that their punches did not break her down, they thought of something else. The only way to break a woman.

"Take off your dress," one said.

Her heart beat fast. She knew she would die and begged her god for a quick end. She shivered, not because she was cold but because she now knew what it meant to fly too close to the sun. She thought back to her primary school days, learning Greek myths about some boy named Icarus. She never found the story believable, and now she could finally pinpoint why she couldn't suspend her disbelief. Her last thought before she blacked out from another kick to the head was that only women are punished for flight.

III.

When Gusheshe regained consciousness, she was alone. She removed her blindfold, barely seeing out of her swollen eye. She was at a sewage pump on the outskirts of town. She willed her battered body to crawl through grass and dirt to the main road. She cried out for help, but her throat was sore. Finally she heard the voices of passersby and thought of the parable of the Good Samaritan. She was saved. She reached out to them for help.

They screamed.

Maybe she would have been saved if the female body were not a terrifying thing. When the passersby saw a naked woman crawling through the grass, they were ashamed first and afraid second. They did not see her bruises. They saw a muroyi. Everyone knew that witches who flew for too long fell out of their winnowing baskets when day broke. The sunlight starved them of their power.

"Muroyi adohna!" a little boy screamed, pointing at her nakedness. "A witch has fallen from her basket!"

And that was her death sentence before the first rock from the growing mob hit her.

Orange & Egg

Which came first, the orange or the egg? In eSwatini, the egg comes first. A young woman lies on her back with her legs spread. The examiner, an old lady with dirty fingernails and a hard look about her, shoves an egg between the girl's legs. If the egg goes in, she is not pure and her family will be fined a cow by the chief for not keeping a better eye on their daughter. The young woman closes her eyes and says a prayer. Her boyfriend is big but not that big. Perhaps the egg will crack.

The examiner gives no thought to the girl's comfort. After all, the old woman has a line of other girls and families waiting for the test. The examiner shoves with all her might, the girl winces and yelps and is ignored. The egg of purest white ruptures into egg-yolk yellow.

The girl has passed the test.

She is rewarded with an orange. When she leaves, she parades the fruit around the village for everyone to see. Bear witness to the fruits of my virtue, her wide smile says. Everyone *must* see the honor she has brought to her family.

Spirit Husband

If your brother kills another man, you must pay for the crime. That's what sisters are for, right? Currency to bargain with. Your drunkard brother breaks a bottle on a man's head during a fight at a bar. For a week, the man from the bar fights on in a poorly staffed hospital. One night during a power cut the hospital generator, devoid of fuel, fails to kick in, and the machines he is hooked onto pause their one job. He dies while the doctors are occupied operating on another patient by candlelight.

His family has agreed not to press charges. His family is reasonable; they do things the old way.

You, sister of the murderer, are to be married off to the dead man from the bar.

Yes, you are.

Crying won't help. The elders have decided.

The dead man from the bar died without taking a wife. A man who is slaughtered before he knows the comforts of marriage becomes ngozi.

An avenging spirit, do they not teach you anything at school anymore? To appease the ngozi, you must be his wife.

He will be your spiritual husband.

On the day of the funeral, your mother packs your things. A pink shirt with Hannah Montana's face on it and some jeans. You are to live with the dead man's family now.

Don't sulk.

You are helping your brother. Otherwise he and the children he will beget will be haunted by the ngozi for eternity.

Do you want the family line to be cursed?

No. So be a big girl. You are married now.

You have to be a wife until you die, of course.

Forget school. From now on you will clean the dead man's family home, cook sadza for his mother, hand-wash his brothers' clothes, dust the furniture, and rotate between members of his extended family's homes, for someone always needs an extra pair of hands. Wear black, for you are a widow now. Burn the pink Hannah Montana shirt.

And then when you die, another girl from your family has to take your place.

You are thirteen.

Soft

A good wife works. Not in an office, for that is unthinkable, but with her hands down a sink, gripping a gardening hoe, scrubbing floors, bearing children.

Boyfriend and girlfriend hold hands and walk down a Bulawayo city street. They must be careful, for public display of affection is still a crime. An officer could walk up to them and arrest girlfriend for prostitution. Boyfriend tenderly strokes her palm. Girlfriend smiles up at him. Soon he will be going to university to study actuarial science. She is lucky to have him, everyone reminds her. He frowns at her hands.

"What's wrong?" girlfriend asks.

"Your hands are still soft," boyfriend says. "And your knees are brown-skinned, almost yellow."

Girlfriend keeps her eyes on the ground.

"Your hands should be hard and your knees dark," he says. "This just tells me you don't do work. Girls that scrub floors and peka isitshwala have dark knees and hard hands."

Girlfriend laughs awkwardly. "When you're an actuarial scientist and we are married, you will buy me a vacuum cleaner, a washing machine, and a dishwasher so that I don't have to have rough hands."

Boyfriend's frown deepens.

"To buy a washing machine is to spoil a woman," he says. "She will forget her place." He lets go of her hand. They walk in silence the rest of the way.

Closed Casket

It's not only men who can fix their partners. Women can, too. A woman barred from working by her husband (for working women are way-ward) finds much time during the day to sit and stew. Her husband, whose children have broken and bloated her body until her beauty has faded, tells her she has let herself go. She turns over the phrase this way and that like a dirty doormat. *Let herself go.* As if she has anywhere to go, she snorts. Her life is one of chains lived behind the bars of a respectable household.

I will fix him, she swears on her portrait of a bloody Jesus Christ bearing a crown of thorns. She hung the portrait in the living room the day they moved in as newlyweds. Jesus, take the wheel and protect my marriage, she prays to the picture every morning.

While she implores Jesus to take the wheel, her husband comes home later and later until he barely shows up at all. He takes up with a slay queen. Her own daughter shows her the social media photographs of the slay queen on a shopping trip in Dubai. All paid for by the wife's husband, of course.

I will fix her, she says. I will fix her good.

Jesus is too slow in intervening, so the wife turns to other venge-ful gods. African gods who dispense wrath quicker than vending machines. The wife visits a muroyi, and the muroyi does what varoyis are said to do.

The vengeful gods are swift. As soon as the husband pulls out of the slay queen, her womanhood moves from its spot in between her legs to her forehead like a third eye. The man screams and runs away, scared of the thing he licked only moments ago.

After a month of penitence he can't help himself and takes up with another slay queen. Slay Queen Number Two's skin has a transcendent shine to it. The wife begrudges her that skin, that light skin that makes men weak in the legs. Slay Queen Number Two, the wife is sure of it, will convince the husband to divorce her. So the wife prays to bloody

Jesus in the morning, but at night under the cover of darkness she seeks out the vengeful gods.

Slay Queen Number Two is found dead the next day. Her once beautiful skin is flayed pink like plucked chicken. They bury her in a closed casket.

Red Hot Chili Peppers

The first flow of blood never announces itself; it arrives an unwanted guest that promises to drop in every month. The first visitation is catastrophe, a gong sounding the doom of womanhood. At exactly noon a gong sounded for a girl in Harare. It is too shameful to tell her mother that the time to dance to the music has come, so she walks all the way to her aunt's house. Look what I have done, she says, taking off her bloodstained underwear, holding it, head hung, towards her aunt.

Her aunt escorts her back to her mother's house. It is the aunt who explains to the mother that her daughter can finally hear the chords and has joined the dance. The mother leads the girl to the bathroom and teaches her how to wash off the blood. As the girl dries off, her mother tells her to lean back against the tub with her legs open. The mother rubs chili peppers in between the girl's legs.

"Now that you are a woman," she says, "this is what happens if you open your legs."

The peppers sting. The girl cries out—an overplayed melody.

She always sits with her legs closed tightly now. It could be worse, her mother told her. Across the ocean in Nepal, girls with blood are forbidden from sleeping inside the house, so a shed, akin to a dog's kennel, is built for them outside. Sometimes in the winter the girls are dragged away by Himalayan wolves.

Dry

It is nothing new for us women to try something daring to keep the interest of our men. If we lie down like a log, we tell ourselves, they will get bored and look for other women who can please them. We scan blogs, buy books, listen around campfires for tips and tricks. Even when most of our partners cannot be bothered to bring us to climax, we search the web and unpack old wives' tales for how to deepen their pleasure. One such tale that women whisper to each other after church and at tea parties finds our ears one day.

Men prefer it dry.

Our wetness is like sandpaper to them. We must start drinking a potion that makes *it* dry.

We quickly hunt down where to find this magic potion that makes it dry. In the public toilets near Bulawayo City Hall, a woman sells the potion we need. We know those toilets. No running water has flowed through those taps. Kombi and bus drivers shit on the floors because the toilet bowls are already piled up. The floors overflow with piss.

But if the potion will make our man quicken to pleasure, we will walk through a public toilet for him.

We walk past the women's clinic in the direction of City Hall, ignoring the posters tacked to the clinic's walls warning of the growing number of women diagnosed with cervical cancer in the region. Sure enough, we find the woman in the public toilet. The potion we buy from her is even smellier than the toilet. Later that night after a bath, we rub it onto our womanhood and pray it makes us dry.

The Pulling

I was watching *SpongeBob SquarePants* the day my gogo knocked on our front door and entered without waiting for a response. She carried with her a small suitcase, a hand on her hip, and eyes that darted from ceiling to carpet scanning for a single speck of dust. Nothing missed those eyes. I almost cut short the last years she had left in her when I engulfed her in a tight hug. I withdrew instantly from her, holding my breath. There was something unusual about the way she smelled that I couldn't put my finger on. She usually had the smoky aroma of food cooked over a fire—she refused to let my parents install magetsi on the farm because electricity makes women idle. Today there was something else mingled with the smoke. I tried to pinpoint what that smell was as she drew me back into her embrace.

"I have come to do what must be done," she said.

For me, turning twelve wasn't a bridge that I skipped happily across to the other side but a tightrope onto which I was thrust. The next morning when I was in the bathroom, Gogo barged in with her suitcase. The sound of the zip opening cut through the air. Inside her suitcase were all manner of herbs, strange liquids, and lotions in repurposed Vaseline bottles. The horrid smell that I'd picked up when she hugged me was coming from the suitcase.

"It must be done before your first period," Gogo said. "For you to become a real woman."

What I remember is this:

Gogo telling me to lie down in the tub. That I must do this before every wash when she is gone.

Gogo rubbing the ointment around her hands, grabbing hold of my legs and pulling them apart.

Gogo smearing the ointment in between my exposed legs and then tugging at my labia, gently at first, like a slight pinch, until each tug became a vigorous pull. I screamed, but her hold on me tightened.

"Kudhonza hurts more if you resist," she said. "We have to pull until it is the size of an index finger."

A pain I'd never known before took me into its arms and refused to let go. I wilted, losing the will to scream. It was not the pulling that was the most excruciating, it was the inability to stop the invasion of my body, the gripping of my loins like they were elastic, the stretching like the milking of a cow's udder.

The only explanation she gave me was "This is for your future husband."

Hole

Which came first, the orange or the egg? Sometimes oranges turn into holes.

After the big white wedding, the groom's mother lays down a bleached white sheet on the marriage bed. Girls these days aren't like my generation, the mother-in-law thinks, they are crafty little things that can cheat even the sure science of an egg test.

The newlyweds are to spend the wedding night under the groom's parents' roof. In the morning, the groom's mother inspects the sheet. It is still white. No blood. If the bride isn't a virgin, she might as well be a hole, a cesspit that's open for all to shit in. The mother-in-law will not stand for a cesspit of a daughter-in-law. She snatches the sheet from the bed and cuts a circle, a gaping hole, into the sheet. She parades the sheet of shame to the guests inside the house, outside to the neighbors, to the street vendors selling overripe fruit, to anyone with ears to listen. She marches with the sheet to the bride's parents' house, an excited mob growing and trailing behind her.

When she reaches their gates, she holds up the sheet like a trophy.

"No blood on the sheet," she shouts to the bride's parents. "Mwana wenyu akaboorwa." Your daughter is a hole.

And now the parents must give the mob their daughter's head.

Plumtree

Marulas and wild plums grow abundantly in Plumtree, a small town whose only elegant feature is the main road that runs through it, connecting the border town to Botswana. A young woman from the big city marries a boy from this small town. The newlyweds pay the parents a visit, as is customary after a white wedding. The couple enjoy dinner and conversation with the groom's parents. They are good, humble people, these parents. The bride already feels welcomed into the family. When the derere and sadza have settled into their bellies, the mother-in-law exclaims that they do not have dessert prepared. The father-in-law tells his son to drive to the nearest store, along the main road, to get them something sweet.

When the son leaves, the mother with a kind smile asks her new daughter-in-law to go grab a shawl from a closet in her bedroom. "I get the shivers at night," the mother-in-law says.

The bride, a good daughter-in-law, dutifully goes to her in-laws' bedroom to retrieve the shawl. As soon as she steps into the bedroom, the door shuts behind her. Her father-in-law is behind her.

"This is our tradition," the father says. "I must test you out before my son can have you."

"I don't understand," is the last thing she says before the test.

The son returns. What he carries away from his parents' home is not what walked in just a few hours before.

"I didn't know of it," he says in the car. He had been educated in the city and received a scholarship to study abroad. He was never around Plumtree long enough to know of these things. Never spoke of wedding customs with his married sisters, his married best girlfriends, his exes, his mother, his cousins, his aunties, the lady selling mangos at the street corner, that woman on the bus with a doek on her head and her eyes on the ground, the cashier at TM Supermarket, the bank teller at Standard Bank, the news anchor on ZBC News, the girl he sat next to in the lecture hall, the girl he tried to sleep with in the dorms but she refused because it would mean her head and he got angry and called her a prude, the girl he whistled at with his guffawing group of friends as she walked alone and frightened to the shops, the girl he chided for having soft hands and light knees, the girl he told "I will be gentle" and never texted back who ended up dead on the news.

The following year, when the couple's first child is born, he holds the baby still slimy with birth blood in his hands.

He thinks, *I don't know if this child is my son or my little brother.*

By the Bottle

I.

There is an old lady in a forest who sells lightning by the bottle. Drop five dollars and you can strike whoever you choose. If the men in

Parliament had any sense, they would abandon their futile plans of trying to make the country a nuclear power by 2030. America will never allow it. If the men in Parliament had any sense, they would send a delegation to the forest, where they would remove their shoes at the door, cross a threshold of salt, and come out with lightning for the army.

II.

A pregnant woman cries all night looking at an image of an ultrasound. Those patches of black and white pronounce a life sentence.

"Where is a son?"

"Where is a son?" she screams at the doctors.

She cries not because she wants a son but because she doesn't want a daughter. Soon a daughter will be born and someone will tell her that her hands are soft and rub chili peppers on her as if dressing a wound and she will learn that eggs are not only for breakfast and she will go to Plumtree like her mother before her and come back a dead thing.

The pregnant woman burns the ultrasound and remembers the way to a naked old lady in a forest.

"I need protection for my daughter," the pregnant woman says to the muroyi.

"From what?" the old lady in the forest asks.

"Everything."

The muroyi smiles a knowing smile. Out of her bag she takes out a clear jar that must have housed sun jam in the past. Inside the jar the sparks dance in a zigzag. The pregnant woman holds a storm in her hands.

"It is bottomless," the old lady says.

III.

When the daughter's breasts bud, an uncle does what uncles do and reaches to pluck a flower before the bloom. It is dark, the government has cut the lights for twelve hours again, but white light surrounds the uncle and flames erupt from his chest. Three times someone tries to beat the flames with a blanket. Three times the flame reignites. An autopsy is conducted.

Cause of death: *Electrocution. Deceased probably put his finger in a light socket.*

There is an old lady in the forest who sells lightning by the bottle.

The Friendship Bench

The young woman is driven to my Healing Hut by a question. She doesn't need to ask it. Everyone who seeks out my services comes here as a last resort.

As soon as she closes the door, the floor beneath her sneakers morphs into a meadow. She inhales sharply, realizing that she now stands in grassland awash in the afternoon's yellow glow. She turns back frightened, looking for the door she entered through, but finds nothing.

I wave at her from the bench under the shade of a jacaranda tree. The purple jacaranda petals occasionally fall onto my graying Afro. The Friendship Bench looks like any other classic park bench, yet the girl hesitates to join me. I smile. It does the trick to persuade her that I look like I could be anyone's grandmother. Good. She'll bring me closer to my quota.

Her name is Khaya. She has come all the way from America. Her life flashes before me like a collage of photographs the moment she steps into the Healing Hut.

"Are . . . are you the n'anga?" she asks in broken Shona. "Makadini zvenyu." She struggles through the greeting.

"You can call me Healer, if you like," I say in English.

Khaya exhales gratefully. She chooses to sit as far away from me on the bench as possible. Most people do.

I know what's troubling her. I see the two branches of her family tree. An African American father and a Zimbabwean mother. Other people have generational wealth, but for someone like Khaya all she has inherited is pain. The pain is a centuries-old, pallid, undulating mass sitting on her shoulders. It is no wonder she slouches so much.

A memory floats in the air as she shifts uncomfortably on the bench. A fight with her father the night before she boarded the plane to Zimbabwe. Her father is part of the anti–Friendship Bench movement.

"It is running away from your problems," her father said vehemently as she packed her bags. "Don't you see that it makes you forget your pain? Your history? It makes you forget the truth of this world. It makes you live a lie."

"Maybe I just want to breathe sometimes," Khaya shot back. "Maybe I don't want to shoulder all this grief. Maybe I just want a life where history means nothing to me!"

The memory disappears with the wind.

"What is troubling you, my child?"

Memories inundate the air. The mass on her shoulders bellows at me, sinking its talons deeper into the girl's shoulders.

"I want you to unburden my soul."

"Very well."

Her eyes widen. "Can you do it? Can you take it all away?"

"Every emotion and sensation, good or bad, that you feel is energy," I say, assuredly. "A Healer's duty is to turn the energy that burdens you into something . . . more pleasant."

I extend my palm. Khaya peers at the device in my hand as if it is a treasure beyond her reach like window shopping at an upscale boutique.

"This is a shock absorber," I say with a smile. "I will implant it in your temple. The device will absorb your pain, converting it into a new energy called an aura."

Khaya's fear and doubts prickle against my skin.

"First you must choose an aura," I tell her. The menu of auras is listed outside the Healing Hut's door. It is the first thing one sees before entering.

"I . . . I . . . don't know," Khaya says. "Can you explain what each aura will do to me?"

"If you choose Euphoria, each time you feel sad, angry, or hurt, the shock absorber will turn it into a state of intense excitement and happiness," I say. "Laughter will make you laugh off every hardship, every hurt. Patience means you will always keep your cool. With Resilience, you will still feel the pain, but it will make you stronger. If you choose Apathy, you will be indifferent to anything that happens to you."

Khaya bites her lip. She can hear her father's voice warning her about the evils of the Friendship Bench. *Don't you see that it makes you forget your pain? It makes you live a lie.*

Another memory escapes from her mind and fills the space between us—Khaya watching the grief eat away at her father, grief that could have been taken away easily by this simple procedure.

"What do you recommend?" she asks.

"I cannot make that decision for you." Her shoulders droop lower at my words. "Most people choose Euphoria," I offer.

Khaya turns over the options in her head. Apathy is very tempting, even Resilience, but she sees no joy in them.

"Euphoria," she says finally.

I lean towards Khaya, tucking her braids behind her ears. I gently insert the device into her skin. All she feels is a slight pinch. When I'm done, the top half of the device sits behind her ear. "All set," I say, leaning away.

The mass on her shoulders blanches until it fades away, melting into a warm sensation. Only one memory remains. Her father is teaching her to ride a bike. Khaya falls and scrapes her knee. Her father is by her side immediately.

"You know why your mother named you Khaya?" her father says in a soothing voice. "It means 'home.' No matter how far you go, no matter how far you fall, you will always have a home."

Khaya smiles for the first time since stepping into my Healing Hut. She has the most dazzling smile of all the people that have sought my services.

"I wish you all the happiness," I say, watching her leave.

The meadow wanes with her receding footsteps and completely vanishes when she is gone. I deposit the cold memories in a jar. My hands tremble more with each new patron, but I can't stop. One more patron and the masters will be pleased. And I'll be free.

Water Bites Back

Only a fool tests the depth of the water by stepping in with both feet. You've always believed this tsumo, always believed that those who don't reason find themselves sinking into a dark cenote of the mind where nothing thrives. You are a member of Parliament, a minister with a very important job, without time for groundless rubbish. You pride yourself on being a practical man. So when you receive the initial reports about workers at the hydroelectric dam project refusing to go back to work due to multiple sightings of a freshwater carnivorous creature, you chalk it up to the workers being superstitious Africans. You fire all the indigenous workers and hire white Africans who, in your view, aren't prone to the irrational melodramatics that your own people often succumb to.

A week later, when the corpses of seven white construction workers wash up near the incomplete dam, everyone else on the team quits. You are under pressure from the president to get this damn dam done, so you put together a task force of reasonable scientists, engineers, and military men, and you drive out of the capital city to the remote town of Lupane to see for yourself what the hullabaloo is about. The white workers are too traumatized to make any sense when probed about what they think happened to their coworkers. The now out-of-work

African workers refuse to talk at all about what they saw. They only tell you to visit a sect of shamans in the area.

"The hydroelectric power plant will benefit this region," you say. "No more power cuts, no more fetching firewood to cook, no more nights lit by candlelight. Can you not see that building this dam is a good thing?"

You have rehearsed the talking points multiple times before meeting with the shamans. You know that these traditionalists are hard-headed, too set in their backward ways to modernize and develop, too stuck in the past to see that there is a future ahead of them if only they could leave superstition behind.

"You forget that we are not the only inhabitants of this region," Anoona says. "When you think of progress, you think only in terms of human progress, but what of everything else? The forests you will flood with this dam, the wildlife whose homes and waterways you will disturb and obstruct."

You're unable to hide your disdain for Anoona, the leader of the shamans, whose locs sweep all the way down to the mudcloth-covered floor. You fume at the indignity of having to consult an uneducated woman dressed in red robes who lives under a thatched roof.

"So what are these creatures in the water? Some sort of wild animal?" you ask, losing your patience. "The workers think they saw something human or fish."

"Just because both a bat and an eagle have wings," Anoona says, "does that mean they are both birds?"

Anoona's apprentices, young women in red robes who sit beside the shaman palm-rolling her locs, giggle at her retort.

"They may have hands, eyes, and hair like humans," Anoona says. "They may have gills and tails like a fish. But that does not make them human, nor does it make them fish."

"Listen, I'm on a deadline here," you say. "How do we get rid of these things in the water?" The president wants his election promise of reduced power cuts to be delivered, and your job security depends on this project.

"Where the water is, Minister," the shaman says, "there must the land obey."

You blink stupidly at the shaman. If slapping someone were socially acceptable, you would have given her cheek a good one by now.

"You were taught in school that the surface of the planet we live on is seventy-one percent water, no?" Anoona says. "By that logic, do you really think it is land creatures who rule this planet?"

The shaman fingers her necklace, which is so intricately woven that it forms a shawl around her shoulders. The necklace is a patchwork of cowrie shells and beads. The shaman takes a patient deep breath before continuing.

"They are called the njuzu nation," Anoona says.

"And what do these njuzu have against dams?" you say.

Anger flashes for an instant in Anoona's eyes, but it passes as quickly as it appears. She takes her hand off the necklace.

"I can conduct an appeasement ceremony on behalf of the government," Anoona says.

"The government has done nothing wrong," you interject indignantly. "We are simply using the resources of our native land to improve the lives of our people."

"There is a pact made long ago between the njuzu nation and our people, long before the whites colonized this land, long before our people forgot to respect both the spirit world and the natural world and the beings that live in between the two. Long before our leaders forgot the blood pact we made with the njuzu nation. This dam of yours is a betrayal of that treaty."

You are so astounded that all you can manage is to croak out a laugh. "Where is this treaty? There is no written record of—"

It is the shaman who laughs this time.

"Written record! Look how they colonized knowledge, and you are the perfect parrot to sing their so-called logic. The treaty is in plain sight and you can't even read it."

You wipe your glasses and peer at her necklace as if you are seeing it for the first time. You have always been good at math and computers;

making sense of ones and zeros is for you an artform. It dawns on you that there is a pattern to how each bead and cowrie shell is positioned. There is some code to the design that you can't quite crack.

"Is that . . . is that some sort of Morse code around your neck?"

"You dismissed my necklace as an adornment with no signification or sophistication to it," Anoona says. "It is the treaty that the njuzu nation signed with us, Minister. It is the treaty that you have broken by trying to restrict the flow of their water with your stupid dam. Then you hired those white workers that thought they knew everything and had no respect for the water. No matter how sharp your teeth are, you cannot bite water. Water bites back."

I am because we are, and since we are, therefore I am. We watch as the shaman leads a group of men to the water. Some of the men carry the fire sticks the humans use to slaughter each other. The metallic sticks glint in the moonlight. It is midnight as time is reckoned on the surface. We marvel at the certainty the humans carry themselves with, like they believe this world was molded just for them. They are but a single grain in an infinite desert of spirit, yet they believe the ground they walk on is solid, that everything they perceive is the beginning and end. They do not see the in-between, do not respect the spirit of this world. They don't see how this entire universe is a web, how a spider dancing on one end sends ripples threading through the silk. The humans from the old world understood this; who do you think taught them that I am because we are, and since we are, therefore I am? It was a hard truth for them to absorb, so they broke it down into one simpler word. They called it ubuntu. But now ubuntu is forgotten. The humans of the old world were deemed savages by the humans from the new world. They were bound and packed on boats and taken away. The ones that remained have corrupted memories and shame like a sickness that compels them to forget spirit.

But there are some among them who remember the old ways, some that have been gifted with the sight to behold spirit.

The shaman carries a calabash of beer, takes a sip, and offers it up to the water. She kneels in the shallows and takes a bite of raw meat, beckoning to us. She sings a sweet song, a song that we taught her. We swim towards her. She touches her necklace and reminds us of the treaty. She apologizes on behalf of her people. We like this woman of the surface. She has kept our waters clean from the plastics that poison us. She has the sight.

The shaman tells us that the leaders of her people have a request. They want to choke up our water. We refuse, shriek in response at the audacity.

The men with the sticks let fire rain on the waters. The shaman screams, jumps in front to shield us, but is caught in the fire. She drops into the water and breathes her last.

"Kill them! Kill them all!" a man shouts.

We lose many to the fire.

For the first time in your life, you turn to impulse before reason. You test the depth of the water with both feet.

"Kill them!" you shout. "Kill them all!"

Those dreadful things in the water cannot be reasoned with. They are animals—unnatural ones, but animals nonetheless. You tell yourself you made the right choice. You nearly vomit thinking of how the shaman appeased the creatures by eating raw meat, bloody and red, straight from the butcher. She said that's how the njuzu like their meat, said doing the things they do would be a sign of respect. You didn't mean for the crazy woman to die, but she jumped in front of the creatures to protect them from the firing squad. The way she absorbed the bullets into herself, it was as if she were receiving a gift. She was unafraid, and was that a glint of pride you saw flash in her eyes before the light blinked out like a power cut? That look will haunt your dreams for months.

The creatures will also haunt your dreams. Olive scales platted across a fish tail, hair mossy and matted like free-form locs, dark pupilless eyes, triangular razor-sharp teeth like a piranha, dark skin that gleams gold in the moonlight.

The dam and the hydroelectric power station take five years to build. At the opening ceremony, you give a rousing speech and the president cuts a ribbon. There are cameras and cheers for progress. There is talk of how the country is catching up to the West.

Your doting wife and daughter are present. They are proud of you.

You look out at the water with unease. You know that the survivors of the massacre are out there.

The humans of the old world had a saying. No matter how hot your anger may be, it cannot cook. Njuzu rage is nothing like human rage; it cannot be contained by flesh and bones.

We unleash our fury in floods.

Tourist boats return to the docks empty, the crew and passengers never to be seen on the surface again.

A couple go for a swim; only one makes it back to shore.

Engineers go to work and never come back.

The humans love taking what does not belong to them; we do some taking of our own.

When they hold a big, noisy ceremony to celebrate the completion of their power station that looms over our waters, we wait and watch at the water's edge. We see a young girl. We smell the minister in her blood. We sing a song only for her ears. It is a song that tickles her spirit; it is rope that coils around her and pulls her to the water. The girl leaves the tent where all the speeches and ribbon cutting are going on. Her mother believes she seeks to relieve herself in the power station's shiny new bathroom. We need her to put both her feet in the water. We cannot take a human unless they cross into our world. The song is a sweet salve on her soul. She steps in, and we drag her into the depths.

When your daughter goes missing, you know immediately that the creatures have taken her. You and your wife rush to the shamans for help and beg for forgiveness. The new leader of the shamans is Thandi, one of the girls who'd been palm-rolling Anoona's locs the last time you came here. She has no sympathy for you.

"The njuzu nation do not harm those they have taken," Thandi says. "They have only one rule: If your loved one is taken, do not cry for them."

Something breaks in you, that logic you pride yourself in falls apart, and the careful dam you've built around your mind cracks like glass. You curse at the shaman, weep until your eyes are red and swollen.

Thandi regards you coolly and says, "Your daughter will never return to you."

When you run out of the hut, you run further from your mind. You roam the water's edge the rest of your days searching for a little girl who was taken by freshwater mermaids.

What the shaman didn't tell you is that the njuzu nation will teach your daughter of the spirit that connects us all. What the shaman doesn't tell you is that your daughter will one day return to this world with the gift of healing, like all humans who are taken. What the shaman doesn't tell you is that your daughter will have no memory of her life before she lived with the njuzu. What the shaman doesn't tell you is that your daughter will become the next shaman, that she will teach future shamans how to care for this world, how to tend to its spirit. What the shaman doesn't tell you is that you are because we are, and since we are, therefore you are.

Turtle Heart

There once was a king who ate the heart of a turtle. He ate it raw and marinated in blood. The thing thumped as he brought it towards his mouth, for turtle hearts continue to beat even after they are dead. He dabbed a white napkin at the corners of his mouth as he swallowed it whole.

He wasn't really a king, just a butcher whose turn it was to sit in the big seat. The island had one rule—everyone took turns to lead. The garbageman, the therapist, the florist, even the artist all had 365 days to use their knowledge to improve the island.

This system worked.

The florist decreed that the people would plant flowers and trees every month. The island became the greenest in the whole world. The artist painted a mirror into which everyone could look and see themselves. Everyone felt heard and represented. The garbageman declared every Wednesday a clean-up day. Soon the island had no plastics in its waters, and its beaches were clean. The therapist sat down and listened, offering empathy as she wrote down everyone's problems in a notepad. The therapist gave the list to the next leader, who was a marathon runner, who worked to narrow down the list, one bullet point at a time. The island got better and better and was soon voted Best Place on Earth to Live by those who stopped by its shores.

And then came the day when it was the butcher's turn to lead. Everyone loved the butcher. The butcher had a rough charm that engendered trust. He made rousing speeches decorated in slogans that rhymed and rang in the ears. For some reason, these slogans stuck long after the speech was over. The butcher made a coat of arms, printed colorful T-shirts with his face on them, and required everyone to wear them or else they wouldn't get their food rations. The T-shirts soon became a uniform.

As time went on, the butcher fell in love with the seat so much that he did what nobody else had done. He demanded 365 more days as leader. Soon this turned into five years, five into thirteen, thirteen into twenty-one, and twenty-one into thirty-one. Those who protested disappeared. The butcher swallowed entire families and belched out their bones. The bones were later found at the bottom of the sea. Nobody dared call their deaths the murders that they were. The islanders began referring to the disappeared ones as the sunken ones. Some even mused that the bottom of the ocean was a better place than the island.

The butcher overturned all laws, replacing them with his own. Each castoff law eclipsed the sun. Darkness and a bitter cold settled on the land. All the flowers withered and died, and all the trees were cut down to make the butcher's chair bigger and bigger.

As the years passed, the butcher knew there was one system he couldn't cheat. His back ached, too weak to hold him up straight, and the grays took root on his head. He consulted a medicine woman, who told him to eat the heart of a turtle.

"Turtle hearts are the elixir of life," she said. "That is the reason why turtles can live so long. Some turtles even live to two hundred."

The butcher-king ordered the islanders to capture all the turtles on the island. He ate turtle heart with his poached oysters and caviar, washing the meal down with champagne. Meanwhile his subjects withered away, skin clinging to bone because the farmers and fisherman had become sunken ones. Soon he refused all meat and drink except turtle-heart broth.

On his hundredth birthday, the butcher-king declared his victory over time.

He lived on and on until all those he grew up with faded with the wind, until those born long after he was born also receded from memory, until no one alive ever remembered that he was once a butcher. The butcher held on to the seat until he was just bones. Even now, when you visit the island, you can still find his skeleton there sitting on the big seat.

The Soul Would Have No Rainbow

A rainbow arches in the sky during my grandmother's funeral. My tears must be the rain that invited the rainbow here. I tell it to go away. Its beauty is vulgar on such a terrible day as this. Gogo is buried next to Sekuru, who died five years ago from complications of his injuries during the liberation war. It is a dignified funeral with no fuss. Gogo never liked fuss. After the funeral we go back to Gogo's house. I pass the basement door, my eyes lingering on the locked door that Gogo never allowed me to enter. Whatever secrets the basement holds, Gogo took them with her to the grave. I lock myself in the guest bedroom and take out Gogo's cookbook from the shoebox I hid it in.

The cookbook is the last piece of my grandmother that I have. I hold it tightly to my chest, imagining Gogo's toasty hugs and trying to will her laugh back into my ears. Tears stain the cookbook, for I know I'm slowly forgetting the sound of her laugh.

Gogo's cooking was unmatched. She even bragged that she once cooked for a British prime minister, but Gogo was always prone to exaggeration. Sekuru never denied her outlandish claims. The corners of his mouth would turn upwards into a little smile as if the two of them knew something I didn't. I swallow nervously. I don't know why opening her cookbook feels like I'm walking in on her in the bathroom, like I'm about to see something not meant for my eyes. A photograph falls out from the first page. It's in black and white, of Gogo and Sekuru smiling, a young black couple in colonial Southern Rhodesia.

Last week Gogo's belongings were divided amongst her relatives at the gova ceremony. People are greedy, always eyeing what they can take even before the deceased dies. I'd heard stories of widows who were kicked out of their houses by relatives who claimed possession of the dead husband's house. My relatives had acted no differently when Sekuru died, fighting over his tiny house and even tinier car. Vultures, Gogo called them. She fought to keep the house, angering my uncles, who called her a list of things ranging from hure to muroyi. While my relatives were fighting over Gogo's property, no one paid attention to her musty cookbook sitting on the kitchen counter, so I'd taken it for myself.

The cookbook smells like its age, earthy and comforting. My skin tingles a bit from having it in my hands. More tears stream down my face. On the first page is a note signed by my grandmother.

The soul would have no rainbow if the eyes didn't have tears, Langa. If you're reading this, my mzukulu, it looks like my cook-book has called to you, which means I have passed on. Wipe your tears before reading on, I don't want you staining the pages.

Gogo M.M.W.

Instantly I rub the tears from my face with my sleeve, laughing at Gogo's cheekiness. I frown. How did she know that I would take her cookbook? I turn the page expectantly, hoping to find a food prep method or one of Gogo's delicious recipes, but I am met with the words NOMKHUBULWANE: GOGO MAGERA written in all caps at the top of the page. Below the words is a rough sketch of a praying mantis. The name Nomkhubulwane is unfamiliar to me, but I know what Gogo Magera is. Why would my gogo have a drawing of a creature from fairy tales in her cookbook?

The mantis has prominent front legs, bent and held together at an angle that makes it look like it is praying. The compound eyes on its triangular head are so lifelike that I can imagine it blinking. I trace the drawing with my index finger, thinking of the bedtime story Gogo used to tell me about the illusive creature Gogo Magera. That was when I'd lost my tooth and she told me to keep it under my pillow for the tooth fairy to visit.

"Better the tooth fairy than Gogo Magera," Gogo had said darkly.

"Gogo Magera? As in Granny Snip Snip?" I'd asked. "Is that another tooth fairy?"

Gogo laughed sharply. When she spoke, her voice was a whisper. "The tooth fairy takes and gives you something in return. Gogo Magera, on the other hand, takes and never gives."

I already didn't like the sound of this Gogo Magera creature as I slowly drifted off to sleep.

"Gogo Magera is a praying mantis," Gogo said. "Have you noticed that a praying mantis's legs look like shears?"

"I thought they looked like prayer hands!" I said.

"No, no, they look like shears," Gogo insisted. "Gogo Magera comes while you are sleeping and cuts off a strand of your hair or both your eyebrows with her shears and disappears into the night with your hair!"

I'd bolted up in bed, instinctively touching my face in horror, imagining what I would look like without eyebrows.

"That's why you must sleep with a doek covering your hair," Gogo said, gently pushing me back down onto the bed and tucking me in. "Gogo Magera only cuts people who don't wrap their hair at night."

Gogo patted the bonnet on my head proudly. I breathed a sigh of relief, grateful that the tooth fairy was coming and that I was protected against Gogo Magera.

Looking at the sketch of the praying mantis now, my hands go to my locs and I chuckle. Gogo Magera is just another cautionary tale grannies tell their granddaughters. I wrap my hair every night so that it's not a tangled mess in the morning, not because of some mythical praying mantis. I wonder, why would Gogo have a sketch of Granny Snip Snip in her recipe book?

I turn another page, and a booklet the size of a passport falls out. I know immediately what it is.

"I can't believe Gogo kept this all these years," I say, leafing through the booklet.

The year is 1955, and Gogo is not yet Langa's gogo. She is twenty-five—in mortal years, anyway. She is much, much older than that, older than this patch of sand they call a country. But she can't look down on the humans; after all, she chose to become one.

As a human woman, she works as a cook in the white suburbs. Every day she makes the journey from the slums to the suburbs. She has to walk half the way and then take three buses. The bus always screeches to a halt when they reach the roadblock right before town. Rhodesian police officers order everyone to get off the bus, crinkling their noses at the sea of black faces. Every Rhodesian is taught that the natives smell. Even native shit smells more than white shit, pure Rhodesian shit. The officers would never call themselves white Africans. They are too pure-blooded for such a label. "Rhodesian," however, sounds like the name of a conqueror.

"Passes!" a Rhodesian screams, his spittle kissing the black face nearest to him.

Gogo takes out her booklet. Everything of hers is in order. It has her ID, her job title, and the travel permit to the suburbs.

The two men in front of Gogo in the line are taken into the police van, their pass booklets deemed unfit for them to proceed to the white side of town.

"Purpose of travel?" the Rhodesian barks at Gogo as he flips through her pass booklet, almost ripping apart the pages.

"I am a house girl at Governor Moffat's," Gogo says.

The Rhodesian frowns down at her booklet.

"They are expecting me soon so that I can cook lunch for their esteemed guest," Gogo adds. "The British prime minister."

The prime minister is doing a tour of the colonies to make sure that the Crown's territories are still in order. The name-dropping works. The Rhodesian throws the pass booklet back at her. He can't inconvenience his fellow good Rhodesians and the PM by delaying the arrival of the help.

Gogo gets back on the bus. This is how every morning in the mortal world starts.

Most people from my grandmother's generation burned their pass booklets after Zimbabwe's independence. The painful memories and humiliation of being stopped constantly by Rhodesian policemen were greater than the need to preserve such a historic document. In my hands, the pass booklet looks innocent enough. If you don't examine it closely, it looks like any other passport. The tiny thing feels heavy in my hands, as if it can explode in my face if I hold on to it any longer. Such a small, small thing to have such weight. I carefully place it back between the pages of the cookbook.

"Langa, come eat!" Mama calls out from the kitchen.

I bury the cookbook under the pillows and plushies populating the bed and head to the kitchen. Mama is still wearing all black, her hair hidden under an austere doek. We eat in silence. Mama has been stripped of all joy and rarely says a word these days.

I try to distract her from the pain chewing away at both of us by complaining about my journey back to Zimbabwe from the States. Talking about the humiliation of air travel is an easier thing to do than facing the wrenching knowledge that my grandmother is gone, disappeared forever under the soil, with only a slab of stone above her grave to remind us of who she'd been.

"Can you believe that they took one look at my African passport and dragged me to a back room?" I say, shoving a ball of sadza into my mouth. "They interrogated me for an hour about drugs."

Whenever I recount my American airport horror story, I try to brush the indignation off my tongue so that it comes out more like an anecdote than the humiliation it was. When I was dragged away from the line, the good white travelers sporting shiny blue passports had stared at me as if I were a criminal. I was detained in a cold, dark room when all I could think about was getting back home in time to grieve. An interrogation turned into a strip search. Naked and trembling in an unventilated room, I yearned to jump out of my own skin. If I wasn't me, I wouldn't be treated this way. Only when I showed the Americans my documents proclaiming that I was a student at an Ivy League university did they let me go—without an apology.

"You can never be too sure," one of them said.

My heart races when I think of how I will have to go through all this again on my return trip. I wish I could take buses across the sea. Anything to avoid being made to feel like a criminal.

Mama sucks on her teeth. "They come to our countries like we are a Blair toilet, but they harass us when we go to theirs."

"I'm just glad I got here in time for the . . ." I trail off, unable to say "funeral" just yet, because saying the word will make it real. I quickly change the subject. "I remember whenever we visited, Gogo used to tell me bedtime stories about Gogo Magera. Then she would spend hours in the basement."

Mama stops chewing for a moment, her body tense.

"Did she ever tell you what she was doing down there all the time?" I ask.

"Who knows," Mama says.

"Do you know what a Nomkhubulwane is?" I press. "Is it another name for Gogo Magera?"

Mama chokes on a chicken bone. Her coughs make her heave so much that I think something is going to burst out of her chest. She reaches for the nearest glass of water, her hands shaking.

"Why are you suddenly interested in this?" Mama says. Her words sound like an accusation.

"I'm just curious, that's all," I say.

"Gogo Magera is a children's story, Langa," Mama says. "Nothing more."

I've seldom heard my name since moving to the States. Everyone at school calls me Lana. "Langa" twists their tongues into too many knots for them to bother to learn it. I know Gogo would have been disappointed in me had she known I'd bastardized my name. Gogo named me for sunshine.

"I'm Lady Rainbow," Gogo always used to say. "And you are sunshine."

Mama stands up abruptly, clearing her plates.

"No more talk of Gogo Magera and Nomkhubulwane in this house, do you hear me?" Mama says. "Those stories died with Gogo."

How to Make a Rhodesian

Blue eyes
Water from a spring in the forest, blueberries and yoghurt blended together to make a smoothie, the eyebrows of a Scandinavian toddler

---

British accent
Yorkshire pudding, a biscuit, the beard of a gentleman fresh off the boat from London

---

White skin
Spoiled whole milk

Cruelty
Vermillion, a pebble from a cold land, a piece of wood from a ship, a thorn stolen from a black rose

The prime minister and Governor Moffat enjoy afternoon tea in the garden. The prime minister is visiting the colonies to show his full support behind keeping the colonies in check. He has brought with him weapons to be used to quench the little flames of rebellion amongst the natives.

"I say, Moffat, these scones are delicious," the prime minister says. He rubs his sweaty forehead with a napkin, not quite used to the African heat.

"The natives are quite excellent at making our food," Governor Moffat says. "I'm tempted to take my cook with me when I go back to England."

As the prime minister gorges on the scones, a praying mantis hops onto the back of his breeches and makes it all the way up to his neck. The prime minister is none the wiser when the praying mantis nicks off a lock of his hair with its scissorlike legs. The praying mantis jumps away, hopping back into the grass and darting across the backyard into the kitchen. There the praying mantis morphs into a human woman wearing a cook's uniform. She seals the prime minister's hair away in a mason jar.

When I open another page in Gogo's cookbook, a key falls out. The key chain has the word BASEMENT on it. The basement has always been off limits to me, so walking down the creaky wooden stairs feels like I'm sneaking into Gogo's kitchen to steal Choice biscuits. I pause before the gray door, a place that has been unknowable all these years but now seems to be the last piece of the puzzle that was my gogo. I'm scared to open it. I've always wondered what was behind the door, yet here is my chance to know and I am shaking all over, unable to will my limbs to open it. With a deep breath and hands trembling, I slide the key into the keyhole and twist, and the door swings open.

The basement looks like an abandoned pantry with mason jars lining the shelves.

Gogo heads to a funeral wake at a neighbor's house where the freedom fighters gather at night, the Rhodesians none the wiser. Gogo runs her finger over the red ribbon tied at the gate. Comrade No Rest Muhondo ushers her to the back of the yard where all the comrades are gathered around a fire.

Gogo is a small woman, but she casts a long shadow in front of the sea of hardened faces. They are silent as they watch her dark skin crack like broken glass, an unsettling paleness emerging from beneath. Her short legs elongate, honey brown hair springs across her legs like weeds, a mustache stretches above her lips, and her voice deepens to a British accent. Within moments, the British prime minister is standing before them where Gogo once stood.

"We didn't have enough weapons to fight the British," Gogo says in her new voice. "But now we do. I walked right into their garrison and walked out with most of their weapons in the image of their beloved prime minister."

The freedom fighters erupt into cheers and whistles as they distribute the firearms.

Dear Langa,

You have found the key to the basement at last. You're probably curious about the mason jars lining the shelves. Let me start at the beginning, my sunshine.

I am a goddess. Well, not quite anymore. I chose to be human, you see. I will get to the reason later. You know me as Gogo Mbaba Mwana Waresa, but before I was your gogo, I was Lady Rainbow, the rain goddess. Why would a goddess choose to be human? you may wonder. In the heavens all the gods were arrogant bastards. An eternity is so long. It yields no surprises, no joy, no flavor. I watched the humans, and I wanted to know what it meant to live and to treasure existence because it might end at any time.

So I went down to Earth, and it so happened that I fell in love with a human man, your sekuru. He was a freedom fighter, passionate. All he wanted was to see his people free.

My father, the sky god Umvelingangi, said I would regret my choice. He told me humans were violent, fickle creatures. Still, I would not return to the heavens.

I was stripped of my immortality, stripped of my powers. When I set foot on Earth, I was born anew as an African woman in a settler colony on the verge of revolution. I could never make rain again but, look, I made your mother, who is a storm, and she in turn made you, sunshine.

I was my father's favorite, he still had a soft spot for me, so he left me with one power. Nomkhubulwane, the power of shapeshifting. That is why I told you the story of Gogo Magera, the praying mantis who steals hair from those who sleep without doeks at night. The hairs I stole as a praying mantis—what does the science you learn at the school in America call it, DNA?—are the ingredients I used to make recipes that would turn me into anyone I desired to become. I used the recipes to win the liberation war for our people and never touched them again, locking them up in this basement. If you could have the power to become anyone you chose, would you stay yourself? This is your inheritance. I leave the recipes to you, my sunshine, all the ingredients pickled into mason jars.

Your loving Gogo

Three Deaths and the Ocean of Time

Now

Gogo Pentshisi's house, at the end of a dead-end street, was surrounded by peach trees. It was strange that for a house without a fence or wall, all the trees were still full of ripe fruit. The neighborhood children, high on the euphoria of playing in the streets with their friends, usually stole fruit from every yard they could sneak into. The hairs at the back of my neck prickled. If the children here knew not to steal from Gogo Pentshisi, what did it say about her? When I reached her house, she was waiting for me. Wordlessly she gestured for me to follow her up the driveway, as if she was used to strangers just showing up at her home. Gogo Pentshisi walked with a slight hunch, and she wore colorful beads that dangled over her chest, an ugly sweater that was impractical for this heat, a zambiya around her waist, and tennis shoes.

A neat pile of salt lined the welcome mat at the doorway. She asked me to take off my shoes and leave them outside. Gogo Pentshisi jumped, barefoot, over the threshold of salt. I followed suit, regretting my decision to come here. When my feet touched the hardwood floor indoors, she nodded, satisfied about something. I had a feeling I'd just passed some test.

"So you've come here in search of answers," she said, speaking for the first time.

"Thank you for seeing me," I said. "Dr. Moyo said you could help with my . . . condition?"

I'd woken up in the hospital a few days ago after another one of my blackouts, which had been occurring for a month. My family's physician, Dr. Moyo, had done everything—X-rays, blood work, a brain scan, you name it—yet she could not untangle the medical mystery.

"Look, Nomaqhawe," Dr. Moyo had said. "Physically, there is nothing wrong with you."

"Maybe you need to run some more tests," I said. I was close to tears. "You must have missed something."

When the nurses and my family left the room, Dr. Moyo leaned closer to the bed, lowering her voice to a whisper. "We're calling your condition blackouts for now, but something tells me that these aren't regular blackouts. You told me you see a woman when you black out? Most people don't see anything. Sometimes what ails us cannot be explained by Western medicine. Perhaps African science holds the answers you seek."

Each time I sank into a blackout, I saw a battlefield. The place reeked of burning flesh and blood; gunfire and screams rang in my ears. Each time, I wanted to run, but my feet were stuck in place like in a bad dream. Each time, a woman stood over me, a battle-axe in hand. She pointed the axe towards me like an accusation and said, "Come to the Zamani."

"What is African science?" I'd asked Dr. Moyo in that sterile hospital room. Dr. Moyo was always a little eccentric, but she was one of the most respected doctors in the country. "Are you going to tell me I should drink donkey piss to get rid of curses and demons?"

Dr. Moyo's face remained deadpan, my joke falling flat. "Sometimes what troubles us is something ancient . . . something forgotten."

"So how do I cure something *ancient* and *forgotten*?" I said, punctuating the words with air quotes and an eye roll.

She took out a notepad from the pocket of her lab coat and scribbled something. She tore out the page and handed it to me. "By remembering it."

I looked down at the note. It was an address.

"I've done all I can do to help you. When you're discharged, go find Gogo Pentshisi," Dr. Moyo said.

"Gogo . . . Pentshisi?" I said, eyebrows raised. "Someone named Granny Peaches knows more than you, a medical doctor?"

"She knows more about African science than I ever will."

So here I was, seeking out Gogo Pentshisi because I'd run out of options. I checked the time on my phone. I had to attend a required event for a course I was taking this semester and didn't want to be late. My grades were already slipping, what with the number of times I'd been absent because of the blackouts.

Gogo Pentshisi ushered me to a floor mat. Incense burned on a table in the corner. The blinds were closed, blocking all light from penetrating the room. On the mat were bones, cards, and cowrie shells. Nine cowrie shells, seven bones, and five cards, to be precise. I wondered if the bones were chicken or human fingers. She sat opposite me and put on a feather headdress.

"How do you know Dr. Moyo exactly?" I asked, eyeing the bones warily.

Gogo Pentshisi gathered the bones in her hands. "I helped her with a problem. I help many people with all kinds of burdens."

I wondered what kind of problem one of Zimbabwe's most celebrated doctors would have that she would need an eccentric old woman to solve it.

"Spit," Gogo Pentshisi said. She extended her cupped palms towards me. I stared down at the bones and then at her face and back at her palms again, barely able to mask my incredulity.

"You really don't want me to spit into your hands," I said.

"Spit," she said again, her tone with a sharp edge to it that told me to do whatever this woman asked if I knew what was good for me. "You want to know who the woman with the red axe is, don't you?"

"How . . . how do you know that?" I said. I'd never told anyone about the axe. I'd told Dr. Moyo that I saw a woman when I blacked out, but I'd never told her about the axe.

"Spit."

Reluctantly I leaned forward and closed my eyes as I spat into her palms. My face was hot with shame. If my professors at the National University of Science and Technology of Zimbabwe could see me now, they would laugh me out of academia.

Gogo Pentshisi shook the bones in her palms for a count of ten and then threw them back onto the mat. One of the bones rolled close to my feet. I inched away from it. The old woman peered intently at the bones, which were now drenched in my saliva. She picked one of them up and dropped it into a calabash of clear water. As soon as the bone touched the water, an image appeared. It was of the woman I saw whenever I blacked out. She wielded an axe, coated with so much blood that the steel could not be seen underneath the red. Questions raced through my mind. I tried to rationalize what I was seeing, find some textbook logic I could apply. Magicians were trained to make mere tricks look like the fantastical, like when they told you which card you were holding up, pretending they could read your mind. It was all just theatre, really. I scanned the room, looking for evidence of the crafty trickery.

"I throw the bones to interpret the will of ancestors," Gogo Pentshisi said. "The woman with the red axe is an ancestor trapped in the vast ocean of time."

"Trapped in the what now?" I said. "What does this all have to do with me?"

"An ancestor can impact your health for a number of reasons," Gogo Pentshisi said. "Sometimes it is because they are displeased with you, sometimes it is because they want some wrong that was done to them when they were alive to be acknowledged—"

If what Gogo Pentshisi was saying was the truth, it didn't sit well with me that my health was being toyed with by a relative who was now bones and dust.

"Your ancestor has a task for you," Gogo Pentshisi said. "Your blackouts will not stop until you have completed that task."

The only words my ancestor had ever said to me during my blackouts rang in my ears. *Come to the Zamani.*

The ZUPCO bus back to campus took its sweet time. As it neared the town square, passing the giant statue of a liberation war general with a rifle slung on his back, I thought of my research and the roadblocks I'd been stumbling over. My thesis advisor wasn't too pleased with me, even though I'd given him countless doctor's notes about my unsolved condition. The last time I'd spoken to him, he told me that the reason I hadn't made any progress wasn't because of my health, it was because "writing a thesis on narratives about female liberation war heroes makes for a thin senior thesis." Sometimes I wondered why I'd chosen English and New Media Studies, an underfunded department run by cranky old men.

When I finally walked into the auditorium, the guest speaker was being introduced.

"We would like to welcome, all the way from Kenya, Shingai Njeri Kagunda, the author of *And This Is How to Stay Alive,* a powerful book about grief, loss, and a sister who time-travels to save her brother from death."

The audience clapped and the guest speaker walked onto the stage, the projector screen behind her displaying the title of the talk, "African Time: The Tale of Three Deaths."

"Thank you for that generous introduction," Shingai said. "I was really excited to get this invitation to speak at NUST. I would like to start this lecture by asking a question. Don't worry, it's not a riddle, although most people think it is one whenever I ask it. Perhaps one of you can give me an answer: How many deaths does a human experience?"

I toyed with the question and could not find the answer. I wasn't even sure I understood the question.

"Unless you believe in reincarnation, we only live and die once," someone from the audience called out.

"Not quite," Shingai said.

The image on the projector changed to a black-and-white photograph of a bald man with wire-rimmed spectacles. Next to the photograph was a screenshot of the cover of a book.

"In 1969 the Kenyan philosopher John S. Mbiti published a book called *African Religions and Philosophy*," Shingai said. "There is a section in that book that details an East African concept of time. He argues that time is moving backward, not forward."

John S. Mbiti and his book disappeared from the projector. They were replaced by a flow chart.

"According to Mbiti, time can be thought of as existing on two planes. The Sasa and the Zamani," Shingai said, pointing at the chart.

I dropped my notebook on hearing the word "Zamani." *Come to the Zamani*, my ancestor had told me.

"Sasa can be thought of as the Now. It includes everything in the present and in the immediate past," Shingai said. "The Now includes all those who are alive, as well as all those who are about to be born and all those who have recently died. All of us in this auditorium are living in the Sasa."

Almost without willing it, I found myself taking notes. I copied the diagram that was on the projector into my notebook. The know-it-all from my class raised his hand to ask a question.

"If Sasa is the Now," my classmate said, "how can those who have recently died reside in the Now? They are dead."

"Excellent question," Shingai said.

A new slide appeared on the projector. It was titled "The Three Deaths."

"People who have recently died are kept alive in the thoughts and hearts of people who remember them," Shingai said. "They are not truly dead. They are the living dead because they live on in memory."

I was trying to keep pace with her words, hastily writing down everything she was saying.

"The other plane of time is the Zamani," Shingai said. "The long-distant past."

She zoomed into the part of the chart labeled the Zamani. "The Zamani is where the living dead recede when they are no longer remembered by the living. When the last person who can recall the living dead passes away, the living dead are no longer the living dead. They pass into the realm of Zamani, the realm of the truly dead. Mbiti called it 'the ocean of time into which everything is absorbed.'"

The déjà vu was dizzying. Gogo Pentshisi had used those very words: *the ocean of time.*

"Therefore, the past is something that we are approaching, not moving away from. All of us here will experience three deaths. The death of the physical body is the first. When we are buried, we cease to create new memories and disappear from the face of the earth. Then we are resurrected as living memory in the hearts of those who remember us, as a living dead person. But then a time will come when even this memory disappears, when those who love us die. When the last person with memories of us dies, that is the final death."

Shingai paused to drink from a glass of water. "We see, then, that African time is not linear and there is no future. As we age, we are advancing towards the past, not the future. All of us here in the Now will one day enter the long-distant past. We will all be forgotten."

Dr. Moyo's words came hurtling back at me. *Sometimes what troubles us is something ancient . . . something forgotten.*

I felt sick. The auditorium was suddenly too hot and stuffy. I wanted to run away and retch over a toilet. Time stopped for me. It didn't register when Shingai talked about her book *And This Is How to Stay Alive* in conversation with John Mbiti's teachings. It didn't register when she concluded her talk and everyone in the auditorium gave her a standing ovation. It didn't register when everyone shuffled together and lined up for a book signing.

When I finally came back into the Now, the line was thinner, the auditorium almost empty. I took Shingai's book out of my bag and joined the line. I was still in a daze when it was my time to have my book signed.

"Thank you for coming to the talk," Shingai said. She wrote a note in the book and signed it. As she handed it back to me, I asked, "What if someone living in the Now has to go to the Zamani. How would they reach such a place in time?"

"Well, for that to be possible," Shingai said with a wry smile, "they would have to time-travel."

When the blackouts first started, I stopped going out and spent most of the time curled up in bed waiting for them to happen. It was safer to black out alone in my room than in public. Sometimes the blackouts were rough, like a sudden jolt or push backwards; sometimes they were peaceful, like slowly drifting into a sweet sleep.

After the book signing, I'd gone home to work on some assignments at my desk. Suddenly I felt the drifting, the soft pull towards the blackness. I rushed over to my bed. Having a blackout at my desk meant waking up hours later with a bump on my head from falling backward and hitting the furniture. I'd learned the hard way that it was safer to be in bed when it happened. My eyes fluttered for a while until they eventually closed as I floated towards the dark. When they opened again, I was back on the battlefield, the warrior woman standing over me.

"Come to the Zamani," she said.

I was ejected back to my room. My posters, my desk, the light hanging from my ceiling all came back into focus. I jumped off the bed and put on my shoes. There was only one place I could go, only one place that could give me some sort of answer. I went back to Gogo Pentshisi. If I had a tail, I would have tucked it between my legs.

"How do I make the ancestor go away?" I asked. "How do I make the blackouts stop?"

"I told you before, by completing your ancestor's task," Gogo Pentshisi said.

"How am I supposed to do that? I don't have a time machine to go to the freaking Zamani," I said in frustration.

Gogo Pentshisi stared deep into my eyes for a moment. I squirmed under the intensity of her gaze.

"How silly to think you need a machine to time-travel," she said. "All you need to do is ask time itself to take you there."

Gogo Pentshisi was shaking a winnowing basket that contained bones and cowries shells.

"I . . . how . . ." I stammered. "You're not making any sense."

"Before you ask time to take you to the past," she said, "you must first cleanse yourself for the journey."

Gogo Pentshisi instructed me to give seven coins to seven strangers. After distributing the coins, I bought seven clocks and turned them back fourteen hours. I hung each of them up so that no wall in my room was left bare. It was difficult to fall asleep with the ticking clocks. The next day, Gogo Pentshisi gave me a bag of sand. I was to sleep with it under my bed for three days. When the three days were up, she told me to bring her one white cockerel, alive.

Gogo Pentshisi took back the bag of sand and poured every last grain into an hourglass. The hourglass was so grimy it looked like something someone would buy at an antique store.

"You cannot enter the past without dying," Gogo Pentshisi said. "To enable you to travel to the past, you must have a stand-in, a place-holder in the present."

She held up the white cockerel by the legs. "This is your place-holder. When you come back to the present, your stand-in has to die, and its spirit will go into the past, replacing the vacancy you've left there," she said before adding, "Now we go to the shrine to have a chat with time."

We walked to Njelele Shrine. The shrine was an hour away from the city. I complained about why we couldn't take a ZUPCO bus or umt-shova, but Gogo Pentshisi said such matters could only be handled on foot. She'd also confiscated my phone, so I couldn't even listen to music to pass the time.

"Electronics would only interfere," she said. I didn't ask her to explain what she meant by that.

Njelele Shrine was inside a cave high up in the Matopos Hills. The climb was brutal, the sun relentless and the way slippery. I was surprised by how agile Gogo Pentshisi was for her age. I was breathing heavily and resting in the small crannies along the way, while she was shooting up the hillside as if it were a couple of easy stairs. I guessed she had done this plenty of times before for the journey not to be strenuous for her. Before I knew it, we were on top of the hill and walking into the cave. At the entrance was an assortment of clay pots, beads, skulls of large animals, spears, axes, and cloth.

"These are offerings brought here by people long ago," Gogo Pentshisi said. "Now nobody comes here anymore but me." Gogo Pentshisi swept the dust away from the entrance. "In the old days, rainmaking priests would pilgrimage here and speak directly to God. Now it's an abandoned place, a relic lost to time."

I'd heard all the legends about Njelele Shrine. It was said that Mwali used to speak directly to mankind, that his voice could be heard from a rock in the cave when invoked by the priests.

"The legends say the voice of God has been silent since 1914," I said. "One legend says a soldier stole it. Another says people desecrated this sacred place so much that Mwali left. The other myth is that the British bombed the rock to prove that there was no voice which angered Mwali."

"The voice goes by many names," Gogo Pentshisi said. "Some call it God, others an ancestral spirit. I like to think of it as time itself."

"So the voice was time, not God?" I asked.

"Time is a god in a lot of ways," Gogo Pentshisi said. "It decides when we are born and when we die. Our lives are ruled by it."

"So the voice . . . is still in there? It didn't leave?" I asked, eyebrows raised.

"The voice never left," Gogo Pentshisi said. "Most people just can't hear it."

"Can you hear it?"

Gogo Pentshisi smiled a sad smile. "I'm a ntungamili, one of the last high priests who can talk to Mwali."

She handed me the hourglass. My hands shook as I carefully placed it in my backpack.

"The sand will start descending the hourglass when you cross into the Zamani," she said. "You must be back in the present before the last grain of sand hits the bottom."

Gogo Pentshisi led me into the cave. In the center was a granite boulder.

"Go on, go touch the rock," Gogo Pentshisi said.

I hestitated, overcome by the gravity of what I was about to do.

The rock had a pull to it. I moved forward as if my body had no will of its own. As I placed my right hand on the rock, I faintly heard Gogo Pentshisi chanting in the background.

"Beware," a booming voice emanated from the rock. "Those who cannot return to the present remain in the past forever."

And then I spun around in endless circles like a clock turning backwards.

The Ocean of Time

I woke up with that sinking feeling, as if I'd plunged down the world's steepest rollercoaster. My blurred vision came into focus. I was still in the cave, a puddle of vomit next to me. I retched again, completely spilling the contents of my stomach onto the cold cave floor.

"What are you doing in Njelele Shrine?"

A woman in a shawl with a brilliant gold neck ring around her neck was standing over me. She was holding my notebook, pens, and the hourglass from my backpack.

"You are not a ntungamili," she said. "You shouldn't be in here."

She spoke in rapid-fire Ndebele that I had a hard time understanding at first. My Ndebele was so diluted with English and slang that it wasn't poetic and beautiful like hers.

I scrambled to my feet, my ears popping as if I were on a plane.

"You're a ntungamili?" I said. "I'm from the future. You have to believe me."

"There is no future, only the present and the past," she said. "You cannot come from a place that doesn't exist."

"Right, right, Sasa and Zamani," I said. "Well, this is the past, I'm from the present."

"Why is it that on the day I come to the shrine for guidance from Mwali, I find a strange girl with strange clothing and an even stranger manner of speaking?" she said. She gestured with the objects in her hands. "What are all these artifacts?" she asked.

"The first is a notebook and pen. I use them to write," I said.

The ntungamili cocked her head at the unfamiliar word.

"It's like recording your thoughts and words," I said.

"These are the same symbols used by the white men," she said. If the ntungamili had seen a white person before, did that mean we were in the nineteenth century when the scramble for Africa happened? But white explorers showed up in our lands as early as the sixteenth century. There was no telling what time period I'd landed in.

"In the present we all do it," I said. "Colonization and—um, sorry, I'm using words you're not familiar with."

"So the white men have taken over the land, as I suspected they would," the ntungamili said.

"Yes, they did, for a long time," I said. "Then we fought back."

"What is this thing?" she asked.

"It's an hourglass. It shows the passing of time," I said. "I have to return to the present before the last grain of sand hits the bottom. A ntungamili in my time helped me—"

"The ntungamili is reckless," she said, narrowing her eyes. "You shouldn't have come here. The past is only for the dead."

"My ancestor called me here," I said.

The ntungamili looked at me as if seeing me for the first time.

"Why didn't I see it before?" she said after a while. "You look just like her."

"You know my ancestor?" I said.

"Come, I'll take you to her."

Outside was not the same landscape I'd just walked through with Gogo Pentshisi. There was a military encampment downhill where bare-chested soldiers practiced with spears and shields. The ntungamili led me to the biggest hut in the middle of the encampment. The hut was round with thatched roofing. Guards stood at attention at the entrance. My guide was announced as the ntungamili Thandiwe before we entered. The interior of the hut was covered with carpets. A woman with my face was seated on a gilded stool.

"Has Mwali revealed the whereabouts of my missing husband?" my ancestor said.

"Mwali has given us something else, Queen Lozikeyi," Ntungamili Thandiwe said. "He has brought us your descendant from many, many decades ahead who has sailed the ocean of time to be here."

My ancestor and I stared at each other without uttering a single word. Her radiance was undeniable. Her hair was cropped short, and she had a gold neck ring similar to the ntungamili's. I had the urge to bow or curtsy but just stood awkwardly, puzzling over why no one in the present had any memory of Queen Lozikeyi. How had I not known this piece of history, and why wasn't she mentioned in the history books?

"Why have you come here, daughter of my daughters?" Queen Lozikeyi asks. "Are you here to help us find King Lobengula?"

Finally, a name I actually recognized. I knew King Lobengula from history lessons. His reign started in 1868, but there was never any mention of the name of his queen. It was during his reign that the British settlement began after they tricked him into signing the Rudd Concession, which gave them exclusive mining and settlement rights. Perhaps that was why I'd been called here, to stop the Rudd Concession and white settlement from happening. Maybe this was my purpose. Maybe I'd ended up in the past to stop what was to come. Maybe history could be changed.

"You said the king is missing?" I said. "Tell me, has he signed any treaties with the white men?"

"The king has been missing for a moon now," Queen Lozikeyi said. "I suspect the white men have something to do with this. He welcomed them as friends, allowed them to take from our land, even though I advised against it. Once he signed that treaty, the white men would not stop coming for more. He tried to annul the treaty, and now he is missing. In my husband's absence, I was named regent. The white men have asked to meet with me to persuade me to sign more treaties, as they did with my husband. They claim it will make this kingdom prosperous, it will benefit the people. I know a fruit that has maggots when I see one. I have refused to sign and refused to meet with them. I have ordered them to leave our lands before the next full moon. They still haven't shown any sign of leaving."

"The white men will conquer this land and force their ways upon the people. It looks like they have already started," I said. "Maybe the reason I'm here is to stop them."

"You cannot change the past, child," Ntungamili Thandiwe said. "To do so would break the present."

"So what am I doing here if I'm not meant to help, to change things?" I said. "Your descendants don't even know your name, Queen Lozikeyi."

"Observe and remember," Ntungamili Thandiwe said. "The only thing you will carry back into the present is memory."

Suddenly a young messenger boy ran into the room. He was breathless, barely able to wheeze out a coherent sentence as he knelt on the floor before the queen, face to the ground.

"The white men are coming!" he said. "They have guns."

Queen Lozikeyi mobilized the army, joining her soldiers in defending their home. I thought of the history books I'd read at school and all the tests I'd taken. They never mentioned this as the first battle for independence. They never mentioned Queen Lozikeyi. A woman had led the first resistance against British colonialism, and we didn't learn about it! She was another woman written out of history.

"I should do something to help," I said. "I should be able to use my knowledge—"

"What is past is gone," Ntungamili Thandiwe said. "What is hoped for is absent. For you there is only the hour in which you are."

Ntungamili Thandiwe held up the hourglass. I didn't have much time left.

"I have to take you back to the shrine," she said. "If you stay any longer, you will not be able to return."

"So what was the point of coming here?" I said, tears gathering in my eyes.

"Have you not been listening to what I've been saying?" Ntungamili Thandiwe said.

It was then that everything clicked. I knew what I must do. "Before we go, tell me everything you know about Queen Lozikeyi."

I took out my notebook and began writing, burning every word into my memory.

Now

I limped out of the cave, passing the dead white cockerel on my way out. Gogo Pentshisi was waiting for me outside. We buried the cockerel at the bottom of the hill. I didn't realize I was crying until the soil completely covered the bird. Gogo Pentshisi did not ask me what happened. She only said, "Do you know that your name means heroine, Nomaqhawe?"

"Yeah, so?" I said. "I'm no hero. I went all the way to the past and did absolutely nothing."

"You're wrong," Gogo Pentshisi said.

We walked on until we reached the city of Bulawayo, named after the bloodshed of a long-forgotten battle. Something felt different. I couldn't quite put my finger on it. My feet collected dust as I walked. I didn't notice it at first. The name of the road that led from Matopos Hills back to the city. Wasn't it called the Bulawayo-Plumtree Road? When I looked up at the green street sign at a junction, I rubbed my eyes in disbelief.

"That street sign," I said, pointing. "It says Queen Lozikeyi Road."

"That's what it has always been called," Gogo Pentshisi said.

"But no one knew who Queen Lozikeyi was before . . ." I trailed off. Queen Lozikeyi was no longer part of the forgotten past, she was here in the present.

When we entered the city, we passed a Queen Lozikeyi Primary School and a Queen Lozikeyi Hospital. I saw a man buy fruit from a street vendor with a dollar bill that had Queen Lozikeyi's face on it.

When I reached the center of town, the statue of the general was gone. In its place was a statue that hadn't been there before. I approached the bronze figure and read the plaque at the bottom.

Warrior queen Lozikeyi of the Ndebele people, known for her outspokenness and defiance of the white settlers. When her husband disappeared, the queen served as regent, having silenced a royal court full of men bickering over the position with the words "It'll be better if I do it myself." She led the army in the first resistance against colonial rule in the Anglo-Matabele War of 1896, also known as the Battle of the Red Axe, the catalyst for the liberation struggle. Lozikeyi was buried with her battle-axes.

Queen Lozikeyi stared down at me. She was just as I'd sketched her in my notebook. She was holding a battle-axe and a shield, her face contorted fiercely, as if she were shouting out a war cry. I reached into my backpack for my notebook, but it was gone. Only the hourglass remained.

When Death Comes to Find You

Marange Diamond Fields, Rhodesveld

Takura sifts through the sand. Not even the groan in his belly or the dirt lodged under his fingernails will stop him. His faded yellow hat does a poor job of shielding his face from the sun, so he brings his prosthetic arm to his face. It's only been a month since the local black-smith attached the auto-appendage, after he lost his right hand to the Grootslang in an abandoned mine.

He doesn't have time to grieve the loss. Besides, he isn't the only makorokoza who has an auto-appendage or who has incurred the Grootslang's wrath. All around him the other makorokoza, there must be a hundred or maybe two hundred of them, are also digging holes in the ground searching for the treasure.

At least we still have lives, Takura thinks.

The sound of their shovels fills the once-quiet savanna grass-land. Female traders carry baskets on their heads. They move from makorokoza to makorokoza, selling charms that promise to ward off the Grootslang. They sell other things too—bananas blackened by the sun, red freeze-its, their bodies—anything to attract a purchase by one of the wretched young men who might happen to dig up something worthwhile.

Takura checks his sieve expectantly. More worthless rocks and dirt. Being an artisanal miner is thankless work, but he does it anyway. You never know when the god of luck will sit on your shoulders and you'll strike it big. Every korokoza knows the tale of one such man who'd dug up one of the biggest diamonds to be discovered in the area. It changed his entire life. He was now a bigwig politician enjoying his riches.

I will find something too.

Takura doubles down on his efforts, putting more earth into the sieve. He whistles to distract himself from the sound that won't go away. It's not the ceaseless digging that bothers him. It's something else, something beneath the soil, as if a million people are trapped down there, weeping. Their weeping sickens him. The others call it the makorokoza's curse. They say the sound goes away after you pay the Grootslang's toll. Most makorokozas cannot afford the toll, so drowning the sound with a drink usually does the trick, temporarily anyway. Takura can't even afford a can of beer to do that.

Takura wants to scream at the voices beneath the ground to shut up, but he doesn't want to look unhinged in front of the other makorokoza, so he whistles louder. Takura thinks back to the day he lost his hand and counts himself lucky. He narrowly escaped with his life. The Grootslang, the guardian spirit of diamonds, does not take kindly to those who take precious gems from the earth without paying the toll. If he hadn't been quick on his feet, perhaps he would be one of the unfortunates underground.

Takura is so troubled by the wailing that, at first, he doesn't notice the sparkle amidst the sand.

A diamond!

He inhales sharply when he picks up the gem, rubbing away the dirt around it.

He drops the sieve as he inspects the find, the euphoria dizzying as he tries to calculate how much he could get for this. Takura is about to put it away when he hears the distant whir of an airship. Everyone stops work to look up as the ship closes in.

The balloon-like craft blocks the sun as it hovers overhead, putting everything beneath it in shadow. Takura notices too late that the airship has the Rhodesveld army's seal emblazoned on its side. Noticing the seal too, the other makorokoza panic and make a run for it. Takura stuffs the diamond into his pocket and scrambles out of the hole he's dug. Before he can retrieve his sieve, the airship fires, the bullets ripping into the backs of ten makorokoza near him. Takura's insides turn to mush as he runs in the same direction as the other survivors, but this is a fatal mistake. The makorokoza and traders ahead of him scream in horror as they are intercepted by a group of soldiers with auto-dogs. The dogs' mechanical bodies are a polished silver.

Takura flees in the opposite direction, the auto-dogs giving chase. He scampers past a charm vendor, a portly woman who struggles to run with a tray of unsold beaded necklaces. Not long after he passes her, he hears her scream as the auto-dogs tear into her.

Takura reaches an abandoned mine shaft and dives inside. He listens for the approach of military boots, heart hammering. He reminds himself that he has a diamond, that he will be okay. Surely the gods wouldn't be so cruel as to end his life when all he's ever wanted is in his pocket?

Suddenly a teargas canister nosedives down the shaft, and gas clouds rise around him. He crawls towards the surface, chest and eyes burning. Takura reaches into his pocket and clutches the diamond as if it is the only solid thing in this world. When he emerges from the shaft, his vision is too blurry to see the soldier lifting his rifle. Takura is still clutching the gem when he hits the ground, a bullet between his eyes.

The Wondergat

When death comes to find you, may it find you alive.

The last thing Takura remembers is being shot, darkness, and then waking up here. The air reeks with the sulphur smell of rotten eggs.

He can't tell where exactly here is, but he knows it's underground. He brings his hand to his forehead. There is a hole there big enough for a bullet to fit.

"No, no, no," he screams. A makorokoza should never die before paying off the Grootslang's toll.

It is unbearably hot, and he is chained to the earth and chained to all the people who have been shot dead in front of him. A whip cracks from somewhere. He doesn't see it, but he feels it licking his taut back. Around him, everyone is wailing, wildly scratching at the earth for an escape. Takura picks up a fistful of soil, and it turns to diamonds in his hands. It is only then that he fully accepts where he is. *Fuck! The makorokoza curse.*

He's been so overwhelmed by the wails of the other makorokoza that he's failed to pick up on another sound. A low, rumbling noise like something large breathing.

"Who dares enter the Wondergat?" a voice booms, echoing as if a thousand voices were layered on top of each other.

In the dark a pair of red eyes glint. The speaker is a gray-skinned elephant with four tusks and a giant serpent's body, forty feet long. Takura wants to scream at the sight of the monstrous being before him, but the creature opens her mouth to speak again and reveals a pair of fangs glimmering in the dark. Her open mouth resembles a Venus flytrap.

"You are charged with stealing gems from the earth without paying the toll, korokoza," the Grootslang says, her hot breath hitting Takura like a furnace.

The creature sits atop a stockpile of gemstones and polishes a large diamond with its trunk. It's the same trunk that wrapped around his arm and snapped it off that fateful day he went too deep into the abandoned mine shaft. Takura wants to run away, but he is chained to the ground. He remembers that the legends say one can bargain for one's freedom with the Grootslang by offering her a gem. He reaches into his pocket and pulls out the diamond he found just before he died.

"Please, take this as an offering," Takura says in a shaky voice.

The Grootslang laughs, her laugh something between a vuvuzela, a hiss, and an elephant's trumpet.

"That would work if you were an ordinary human who'd stumbled into the Wondergat by mistake," the Grootslang says. "But you aren't an ordinary human. You are a korokoza. One measly gemstone won't be enough to repay all that you have stolen from the earth."

"I had no choice but to become a korokoza," Takura says. "What options does an orphan—"

"I'm as old as time itself, boy. I've heard every sob story you can think of," the creature says. "None of them move me."

The Grootslang drops the diamond she was polishing onto her mountain of jewels.

"I sentence you to grow diamonds until you've made enough to pay off the unpaid toll you've incurred," she says. "Only then can you have your freedom. Only then can you move on to the afterlife."

Takura remembers an older makorokoza telling him it is well known that diamonds are grown by dead makorokoza. Takura dismissed it as a superstition meant to scare poor orphan boys like him from becoming makorokoza.

"I would have paid the toll, I swear," Takura says, desperately. "I just died before I could—"

"Silence!" the Grootslang says. "I care not for the ramblings of thieving humans. Now get to work. The more diamonds you grow, the faster you can pass on. From the looks of it, you're going to be here a long, long time."

The Kimberley Process Report to the League of Nations
Summary
Twenty years ago, a group of diamond-producing states, diamond industry executives, and activists against blood diamonds met in Kimberley, South Africa, and vowed to keep the trade in rough diamonds conflict-free. Ever since, only member states of the Kimberley Process can legitimately sell diamonds across the globe.

In order for a country to be a member, it must ensure:

i) that any diamond originating in the country does not
   finance a rebel group or other entity seeking to overthrow
   a League of Nations–recognized government,

ii) that all diamond companies operating in its territory pay
   a toll to the Grootslang, and

iii) that the country's makorokozas are protected. The
   willful murder of makorokozas to increase the number
   of diamond growers bonded to the Grootslang is strictly
   forbidden.

This three-step process has rid the world of blood diamonds.

The Kimberley Process Annual Summit, Kimberley, South Africa

The politician reaches into his suit pocket, pulls out his whiskey flask, and takes a quick sip. He looks out the window, barely registering the stunning view of the vineyard. He is acutely aware that he is here to represent his country. The president and the minister of defense have given him strict instructions to get results on this trip.

In the elevator down to the conference room, he recites his speech in his head. His palms are sweating when he shakes hands with diamond industry executives, government officials, and even makorokoza rights activists. He takes his place at the conference table to listen to a robot standing by a podium. She is the leader of a task force sent to investigate the alleged human-rights abuses at Marange Diamond Fields.

"The nation of Rhodesveld is accused of engineering mass executions of makorokozas to increase the number of diamond growers indentured to the Grootslang, thus increasing profits," the robot says. "When I interviewed the survivors of the Marange Massacre, my human colleagues were so appalled by what they heard that they had to leave the room. I present the facts here today."

She fixes her eyes on the politician as she narrates every detail, every murder, every data point she has collected. She narrates how, after shooting artisanal miners dead, the Rhodesveld army brought in prison labor to dig the mass graves. She talks about how each dead makorokoza means higher diamond output for the big companies. She talks about how Rhodesveld's army is the owner of one of the biggest diamond companies in the country. The politician's face does not change, does not betray any emotion.

"The crimes committed by the Rhodesveld army must be acknowledged and must stop," she says. "Until they do, I recommend that the Nation of Rhodesveld be suspended from the Kimberley Process on the basis that Marange diamonds are blood diamonds."

The politician curses inside. He wishes he could smash the robot to pieces, maybe sell off its limbs as auto-appendages. He doesn't betray his rage as he goes to the podium to speak. The politician is a heavyset man, which many people in the room find ironic, because he is one of the leaders of a nation on the brink of starvation. He scratches his mustache before he begins his rebuttal, sweat licking his brow as he remembers the minister of defense's thinly veiled threat about the consequences if he should fail. He is the minister of mines, a cushy position he isn't willing to lose just because a few dirty makorokoza have been killed to ensure the business runs smoothly.

"Your data are wrong. Those testimonies are, without exception, lies told by lawbreakers, lies meant to discredit and undermine legitimate authority in Rhodesveld. Two hundred people didn't die in Marange, only two died, and that's because they trampled each other during a stampede. The army had nothing to do with that," he begins. "The makorokoza are illegal miners who trespass on government property. As soon as security caught them, they fled and trampled each other in a stampede. Rhodesveld complies with all the demands of the Kimberley Process. If the Kimberley Process wants to intrude on a sovereign nation's business, then I must say, without apology, that we don't need you. We will sell our diamonds, no matter what you say."

The European and American delegations shift uncomfortably at the threat. They can't have all those diamonds go to their enemies. Diamonds power airships, robots, and everything else in this goddamn world. If they need to placate a troublesome little African country to get enough diamonds to keep their countries running, then so be it.

"Yes, the mining industry in Rhodesveld is largely controlled by the army," the politician says. "This robot, which I need not remind you is powered by diamonds mined at Marange, wants to suspend Rhodesveld on the basis that our diamonds are blood diamonds, but the Kimberley Process defines blood diamonds as 'diamonds sold by a rebel group or other entity seeking to overthrow a League of Nations–recognized government.' Last time I checked, the Rhodesveld army wasn't a rebel group. The Rhodesveld army is an organ of a democratically elected government, a League of Nations–recognized government. Marange diamonds, by definition, cannot possibly be conflict diamonds."

When it is time to vote on whether Rhodesveld should be suspended from the Kimberley Process, the vote is unanimous. Marange diamonds are not blood diamonds.

The politician exits the meeting with a small smile, careful not to gloat or laugh out loud until he gets to his room. He can relax now. His position is secure. He is about to get into the elevator when the wailing starts, louder than he has ever heard before. It's as if underneath the floor there are millions of people pounding with all their might, screaming to be let onto the surface. He curses and takes another swig of whiskey from his flask. The noise ceases.

The politician hasn't always been minister of mines. Most people don't know that he was once a makorokoza but, unlike the others, he managed to crawl out of the dirt.

Cambridge, Massachusetts

The alchemist opens the door in his kitchen and descends the moldy stairs leading to his basement lab. He changes into a white coat, gloves, and goggles. He can't do this kind of work at the lab at Harvard, because he doesn't want his faculty advisor taking credit for his research.

At the center of the lab is a strange cylindrical contraption that, if it were hovering in the sky, people would call a UFO. A lavender glow emanates from it.

Everything's coming together quite nicely, he thinks. *I won't even need Harvard anymore when I share this with the world.*

He calls the device a diamond grower. He can't think of anything more creative than that. The device mimics the high pressure and high temperatures of the earth's mantle, where diamonds form naturally over millions of years. That's what the science says about how diamonds came to be in this world, but everyone in the diamond industry knows the real truth. The best diamonds grow in Africa because some sort of demon overseer called the Grootslang enchants the process. It is dead humans down there who make the diamonds, until they can pay off their toll to the Grootslang.

If the alchemist succeeds, he will be a true alchemist. He can almost taste the Nobel Prize. He will have single-handedly rid the world of blood diamonds. His diamonds will be ethically and morally pure. No makorokoza will have to be indentured to a demon spirit for diamonds to exist in the world.

An alarm sounds, and the alchemist inspects the device closely, picking up what lies at the bottom with tweezers. He grins and marvels at the little gem he has just grown.

World Diamond Council Headquarters, New York

A small group of diamond mining executives gather around a conference table. The window has a view of Central Park. They've all had a terrible morning, jetting in on their private airships from all corners of the earth for this emergency meeting.

"Airlines across the world are canceling their contracts with us and opting to use these synthetic diamonds for their airships," a British member of the council says, unable to stand the silence around the table. "That's half our target market gone. Who would have thought that some nerd tinkering in his basement would disrupt the diamond industry?"

"Have you heard what they are calling him?" an American asks. "The alchemist."

"There is no need to panic just yet," the council president says, standing before a hologram of a young couple, a large diamond on the woman's ring finger. "This is who we should reach," he says, pointing to the hologram. "Eighteen-to-thirty-year olds. The millennials."

"Who are we kidding?" the Brit says. "The two things that could destroy us all are synthetic diamonds and marriage-adverse millennials. Both are already here!"

"She's right," the French council member says. "When baby boomers were twenty-five to thirty years old, eighty percent of them were already married. Millennials aren't even interested in love, let alone marriage."

"Another thing we're forgetting is that the millennials are broke!" the Brit shouts across the table. "They can't buy diamonds when they can't even afford their rent."

"Indeed, millennials earn less than baby boomers did at their age," the president of the Council says, trying to restore calm to the room, "but our research shows that millennials buy luxury items like iPhones and pet auto-dogs, and they don't hesitate to drop thousands of dollars to travel to another country just for good Instagram photos. So money isn't the problem. We just need to convince them that they should spend on diamonds the money they would have spent on other things. Just as smartphones are status symbols, we should turn a diamond necklace, watch, and ring into status symbols again."

"And how are we going to do that?" the Brit snorts. "The millennials think diamonds are evil."

"And this synthetic-diamond-growing alchemist hipster is marketing his diamonds as conflict-free," another executive whines. "That will surely attract all the millennials. They care about such foolish things, ever since that movie with that blond actor, what's his name again?"

"We need to take back the narrative about mined diamonds," the president says. "My team of researchers have learned that synthetic diamonds take a lot of energy to make, which translates to production of a lot of greenhouse gases. If we release this information, people will be up in arms. They care more about the environment than some poor makorokoza in Africa. The issue of the makorokoza will soon be forgotten."

All the executives around the table nod. Even the Brit doesn't have any snide remarks.

"We need to market mined diamonds as natural, from the earth," the president says. "People will buy a tomato for a hundred bucks if you slap the label 'organic' on it. Why not do that with diamonds? Where synthetic diamonds ruin the environment, natural diamonds are from the very earth we need to conserve. That's why we pay the hefty toll to the Grootslang, the spirit caretaker of the gems, to preserve the earth. That's our message."

"And what about all this Marange Massacre nonsense?" the Brit asks, skeptical.

"Again, we flip the narrative," the president says. "By buying natural earth diamonds, you are helping a poor miner in Rhodesveld. Diamonds uplift communities."

The executives, putting their billions where their mouths are, greenlight the new marketing campaign.

Rodeo Drive, Beverly Hills, California

Hailey walks into Tiffany & Co., the blue of the building's awnings transforming her bad mood instantly. One of her sorority sisters shot down her suggestion this morning that everyone in the house switch to cruelty-free makeup brands. *What a bitch*, Hailey thinks, *what kind of a monster is against cruelty-free products?* But Hailey knows just the right thing to make her feel better. A Marange diamond necklace. They're all the rage these days, plus buying one supports a whole African village or whatever. She got rid of all her synthetic diamond jewelry as soon as the awful news came out that synthetic diamonds kill the environment. Marange diamonds are natural, earth diamonds, given freely by the Grootslang, a benevolent creature that looks after the diamonds underground. Lily-Grace, the influencer she follows, did an informative YouTube video about the history of the Grootslang while unboxing her Marange diamond necklace. Hailey fell in love instantly.

"From our newest collection," the shop assistant says when she notices Hailey eyeing a seven-strand necklace. "Natural, earth diamonds from Marange."

"That name is so cute," Hailey says. "It kinda sounds like 'meringue.'"

When Hailey leaves the store, she has new earrings as well as the necklace.

The Wondergat

There are two things Takura knows to be true. One: Life is unfair. Two: Death is even more unfair.

"When death comes to find you, may it find you alive," Takura says to the korokoza who works next to him, an old man called Sekuru Bob, who was killed at Marange too.

"Reciting old proverbs, are we?" The korokoza chuckles. "Anything to make the work go faster so we can pass on."

"What makes you so eager?" Takura says.

"What do you mean?" Sekuru Bob asks.

"What makes you so sure that what comes after this will be any better?" Takura says. "Our lives were shit. Our deaths are shit. You think our afterlife will be any better?" Takura snorts. "Just listen to the words. 'When death comes to find you, may it find you alive.' I never understood what that means until now. We've never lived, Sekuru. When death came for us, we'd never lived. Do you know who gets to live? Rich people. Those diamond executives, those politicians. The afterlife will probably be nice and cushy for them. We will probably be their servants in the afterlife, polishing their fucking shoes for eternity."

"Come on now, don't talk like that," Sekuru Bob says, patting Takura on the shoulder. "There is hope for a better—"

"The makorokoza are punished for being poor!" Takura says, unable to contain his rage. "We are punished because we are unable to pay the toll to mine the Grootslang's diamonds while we are alive.

Big diamond companies can pay the toll without blinking an eye. When an exec dies, they won't be stuck in this stinking hole. Even the afterlife is made for the rich."

The other makorokoza perk up to listen as Takura speaks. Takura recognizes every makorokoza down here. Some are older men who died years ago. They sing a work song in a call-and-response style as they grow diamonds in time with the rhythm. Takura's outburst is drowned out by their repetition of "Shosholoza."

To pass the time, sometimes the makorokoza argue about the origins of the work song. Some say it's South Africa's second national anthem, but the older makorokoza point out that the song was sung by Ndebele miners from Rhodesveld, who worked in South African mines and travelled back and forth between Rhodesveld and South Africa.

Takura loses track of time. This place is outside of time. He doesn't remember how long he has been here or how much longer he has to grow diamonds until he is allowed to rest.

Shosholoza!

Shosholoza!

Sometimes Takura passes time by talking to the Grootslang. The Grootslang is surprisingly chatty as long as the work is being done.

"How did you come to be?" Takura asks her.

"I am as old as the world itself," the Grootslang says, proudly. "I was created when the gods were young, immature, and inexperienced in the art of creation. After creating my kind, the young gods realized they had made something monstrous. My kind was too much, they said. Too smart, too cunning, too strong."

The Grootslang snatches a diamond in her trunk and squeezes until it shatters into a million pieces.

"The gods liked some parts of their design; they didn't want to completely get rid of us. So they decided to split my kind into two separate creatures. That's how the first elephants and snakes were born."

"I thought you were the only Grootslang," Takura says. "There are more out there?"

"The gods killed my sisters off in a rain of fire. You know that asteroid that killed off the dinosaurs? That was meant for us. The gods said we were too monstrous to roam the earth," the Grootslang says, two tears pouring out of her red eyes that look so much like rubies. "I am the only one that survived, because I hid in the Wondergat. I've been here ever since."

"You are not a mistake," Takura says. "My parents dumped me in a trash can. My whole life I thought I was a mistake, but I am not. I was just abandoned. Now both you and I are trapped here in this dark place. We are more alike than you think."

The other makorokoza continue to sing "Shosholoza."

"It is this world that makes monsters of us all," Takura says.

"Ever since the gods killed off my sisters because they thought we were monstrous, I've made it my purpose to show them how monstrous I really can be," the Grootslang says.

"Why should we be the ones to live in the darkness?" The words tumble out of Takura's mouth before he even realizes what he is suggesting.

The Grootslang flings her massive tail, wrapping it around him like thick vines, and lifts him off the ground, eyes narrowed.

"There . . . there is . . . a saying that abandoned street kids like me used to say whenever . . . whenever people would pass us on the street without offering any help," Takura says, gasping for air as the Grootslang's hold tightens around him. "We would say, 'When a needle falls into a deep well, many people will look into the well, but few will be ready to go down after it.' I've been waiting my whole life for my parents to love me, to finally give a damn about me and come find me. When I realized they were never coming, I waited for some kind stranger to help me, adopt me, anything to lift me out of my misery. Nobody came. Then I waited for the government to do something to help the street kids, to give a damn about us. I've been the little needle stuck at the bottom of the well waiting for someone to give a damn, waiting for someone to stop watching my pain and actually do something to ease it. But I know now that no one is going to do that, so today I choose to get out of the fucking well myself."

The other makorokoza chime in, and a revolutionary fervor sweeps across the Wondergat.

"There is an entire world on the surface," Takura says. "Why should you be down here and everyone and everything else up there? You are the first creation, so smart and so strong that the gods feared you. The gods called you a monster, but what of the army, the diamond companies, and the politicians who murder to fill their pockets? The real monsters are up there."

Suddenly the Grootslang drops Takura and breaks his chains. She breaks every indentured makorokoza's chains. Everyone in the Wondergat falls silent, staring at the Grootslang.

"Is this a trick?" one of the makorokoza asks.

"No trick," the Grootslang says. "You can pass on to the afterlife. Or you can come to the surface with me."

Every makorokoza stays put, nobody passes on. The Grootslang picks up Takura and carries him on her back.

"To the surface, monsters!" the Grootslang bellows.

"To the surface!" the makorokoza yell, their fists in the air.

The Grootslang charges towards the opening of an abandoned mine shaft. She sees sunlight for the first time since her sisters were exterminated, the light almost blinding her ruby eyes. One by one an army of ghosts breaks the surface.

When death comes to find you, may it find you alive.

Drinking from Graveyard Wells

The house disappears on a Sunday morning in April. Mama, the neighborhood gossip, is the first to notice. She wakes up with the sunrise to pin laundry up on the clothesline. Our patch of backyard is a prime vantage point for her to peer into our neighbors' houses, taking note of whose husband is crawling back from a bar or a lover's bed. While craning her neck over the wet clothes, she notices that something is odd, different, misplaced, yet she can't quite put her finger on it. She moves closer to the fence to get a better look, then she finally realizes that our neighbor's house is . . . gone.

The asbestos roof, the incessant coughing that announced that the family of five was awake, the reeking outdoor Blair toilet, the off-white walls, the dirty windows (which Mama always frowns upon because even though we're poor, we should always keep our houses clean) have all vanished. Only the fence, which once surrounded the two-room house, and the rusty address plaque reading *1980 Hopley* remain as markers that a house once stood there.

"Loveness!" Mama screams for me.

I ignore her at first, thinking she is excited again about seeing something she shouldn't have. I concentrate on my math textbook and hit the back of my old calculator so it can blink back to life. I hope this calculator can hang on until the A-Level exams at the end of the year. If I pass my A-Levels, maybe I can get a scholarship for university and get the hell out of this shit town.

Mama runs inside like she is determined to win a gold medal for the country. She shakes Baba awake from his drunken stupor on a mat in their bedroom. She snatches up my little brother, Lovemore, who is wrapped in a bundle next to Baba, and babulas him on her back. Lovemore looks so cozy being carried on Mama's back, I think grudgingly as she charges across the kitchen, which serves as my bedroom at night.

"Loveness, wake up," Mama says, almost tripping over our paraffin stove near the door. "The Moyos' house has disappeared!"

We sprint out of our one-bedroom house, Mama screaming louder than the ill-fed babies of Hopley for everyone to wake up and come see. A crowd gathers outside the Moyos' house which is no longer there. Children point, people stare, mouths agape as if stretching their mouths any further will explain the gap, and Mai Petunia who lives down the street clutches her rosary to ward off evil and exclaims, "Mashura." Senzeni, a boy from my high school, jumps the fence to investigate.

"Hezvo how does a house just disappear nje?" Senzeni says as he walks around the empty spot where a house should be. "Ko where did the Moyos go?"

Senzeni uses this large gathering of people as an opportunity for his small business—dealing bronco and mbanje to numb the onlookers against the reality of living in Hopley. He catches my eye in the crowd and smiles that lopsided grin that I hate to admit is irresistible. He adjusts his bucket hat as if he is self-conscious, puts a matchstick in his mouth, and approaches me.

"Boffin," he says.

I roll my eyes at his nickname for me. Senzeni started calling me that the first time I came first in all the subjects in our stream.

"I still don't understand why you walk around with a matchstick in your mouth," I say to him. "You look ridiculous."

"This world is cold, boffin," he says. "Best to walk around with matches."

Mama grabs my arm, drags me away from him, and hisses in my ear, "I told you to stay away from that tsotsi, Loveness!"

Hastily built one- and two-bedroom houses dot the landscape, popping up daily with no real order or symmetry like mushrooms in the rainy season. Hopley germinated from the rubble in the wake of the government bulldozers razing our old homes because they were eyesores. They called it Operation Move the Rubbish, so I guess to those in the big city we're no different from the landfill, something that everyone knows is accumulating at the edge of the city but no one dares to look at or follow the trail of the smell. I stare at the eerie gap in front of me, trying to conjure the images of Mr. Moyo, his chirpy wife Mai Bornfree who played Mai Charamba gospel songs to the highest decibel as if bursting your neighbors' eardrums was what got people to heaven, and their madofo children who played maflau throwing and dodging balls all day. I've always hated my neighbors for making it difficult for me to study. I've always wished they would disappear. Has my wish really come to pass?

Everyone in Hopley nicknamed their house Independence House because Mr. Moyo never failed to mention that his address matched the year our country gained independence from the British. "All my children are born-frees," he would say proudly. I'd always bite back the retort that being born free in Hopley didn't count for much.

Mama uses the last of her airtime to call the police, but the police officer laughs when he hears which neighborhood she is calling from. The police officer says he will only drive all the way to Hopley if Mama will buy fuel for the police van to come that far.

Eventually people go about their day, spreading their own versions of what happened to the house. I hear a woman by the musika say that Mai Bornfree sings in the church choir, leading praise and worship every Sunday. Maybe her angelic voice stirred God's heart so much that the house sprouted wings and flew the family to heaven. If you look directly at the sun, you can almost see the imprint the alabaster wings made as they pierced the sky.

There is a saying that doing the same thing over and over again yet expecting different results is the definition of insanity. I turn the tap over the kitchen sink thinking that perhaps today will be the day I see a running faucet. Nothing comes out. Maybe I am insane for hoping. I wonder if the pipes feel useless for not fulfilling the only purpose for which they were created. Before I go to school I fetch three buckets, place them on the wheelbarrow, and make the daily trek to the well. Senzeni abandons his corner and runs to catch up with me, offering to push the wheelbarrow.

"A pretty girl should never do manual labor when us gentlemen are around," Senzeni says.

"Are you coming to school today?" I ask, letting him take over.

"Maybe tomorrow," he says, shrugging.

"It's the only way to get out of here, you know," I say.

"Tsotsis belong in Hopley," he says. "You get out. Don't forget me when you're a mbinga."

"You're not a tsotsi," I say. "You were just born in Hopley."

We walk in silence until we reach the outskirts of the neighborhood. We pause before the entrance of Hopley Cemetery. A long line for the well already cuts through the rows of tombstones like a giant tapeworm inching towards its host. Instead of the usual queue chatter about how water only runs once a week now and how ZESA shouldn't dzima magetsi during the Manchester United–Arsenal game or else they will beat up the power station's general manager, people talk about the house.

"This is the work of satani diaborosi," Mai Petunia says, putting down the bucket she is carrying on her head. "We must pray for the Moyos' safe return."

The line is slow to move, and I grow irritated. I will be late for school. I don't want to miss anything, with exams being this year.

"Do you ever get scared?" Senzeni asks suddenly.

"Of?"

"You know," he says, twirling the matchstick in his mouth, "drinking from graveyard wells."

I try not to think too much about the two hand-dug wells in the middle of the cemetery. They were dug by Hopleyans who took matters into their own hands out of frustration with the water shortages. The wells are most likely contaminated with embalming fluids and decomposition.

"I'm more afraid of not having water," I say.

"Maybe that's why the house disappeared," he says, lowering his voice. "The dead are getting their revenge because we're drinking them." Senzeni pushes the wheelbarrow forward as the line moves. "Resting places should never be disturbed," he adds grimly.

"So you think the dead opened up the ground and swallowed the house?" I say, punctuating the question with a giggle so that Senzeni can't see the fear underneath my mask of logic. Senzeni gives me a long, hard stare but does not respond.

The well diggers charge twenty bond notes for three refills.

Mai Petunia organizes a prayer session at her house that night. Mama and I fry some vetkoeks for the event and we all gather inside Mai Petunia's tiny house, some guests spilling over to the veranda which Mai Petunia polishes religiously every morning. Mai Petunia offers us black tea with a splash of lemon. Mama bites into the oily fried dough, washing it down with the tea, and makes a face. "Mai Petunia can't afford milk and sugar," she whispers to me and the woman seated next to us. Our family can't afford milk either, because Mama is saving up every penny for my exam registration fees. I don't say anything, lest I embarrass Mama in front of our neighbors.

In between prayers, Mama offers tidbits of gossip about the Moyos.

"That family has always been odd. One can never trust people who never clean their windows. And that husband, I never trusted him one bit, he had those shifty eyes and never greeted me."

"Perhaps Mr. Moyo vakachekeresa," Mai Petunia says. "People sacrifice their own children these days to make money fast. Eventually the demons come to collect at night."

"That would explain how he got promoted all of a sudden," Mama says, nodding.

Last week Mr. Moyo had been promoted to supervisor at the security company that provides guards for the rich neighborhoods like Borrowdale Brooke. I want to say something, want to tell them that maybe he worked hard for that promotion, but I just sip on the tea in silence, the lemon stinging my tongue.

I'm making biology study notes by candlelight when Mama wakes up two hours earlier than usual to check if the prayers worked. The house and the Moyo family are still gone. When day breaks, she makes her way to Mai Petunia's house ready to imply that perhaps Mai Petunia isn't the great prayer warrior she thinks she is. She doesn't give me the reason why she wants me to come along with her on one of her shit-stirring missions. I guess when you have nothing else to give your children, you give them spite.

"That woman thinks she is Mary mother of Jesus herself," Mama says. "If her prayers are so powerful, why hasn't the house returned?"

Mama is salivating so much at the thought of the look she'll see on Mai Petunia's face when she delivers the blow—"Hamusi kunamata askana. Pfugamai"—loud enough for everyone to hear, that she doesn't notice the anomaly at first. It's only when Mama walks up to knock on Mai Petunia's door that she realizes that there is no door to knock on, for house number 1982 is gone too.

Every day a house disappears in Hopley.

1979. Pretty, the prostitute, and her four children born of men who felt owed and didn't pay. She loved those children like a gardener tending flowers.

1984. Moreblessing, the hwindi who couldn't read or write but could easily count the fare from passengers. He was all gap-toothed smile and smelly breath with a twinkle in his eye that refused to die.

1977. Gogo Mlambo who sold maputi, chips, jolly juice, maveggie, and freeze-its under an umbrella on the sunniest days. She always gave me mbasera with a smile. I would clutch the extra tomato or onion like a precious gift.

1988. Sekuru John whose children all left for South Africa and never came back. He sat by his door every day looking down the road, waiting for them to emerge from the dust.

1975. Martha, Mary, and Matilda. Orphans all below twelve who Mama sometimes checked in on. Smart little things who made a solar lightbulb all by themselves so they always had light.

1992. Mai Memory, a lonely widow kicked out of her home in the nice suburbs by her husband's family before the first fistful of dirt hit the casket. She braided my hair like it was my wedding day.

At school I try to ignore the empty desks where some of our disappeared classmates once sat. Teachers go on strike again, so my classmates and I sit in math class listening to Holy Ten and Winky D, hoping that our teachers will pity us and return to work for peanuts. Once in a while everyone's gaze falls uneasily on the empty desks. Senzeni lights a joint—he is only here because the teachers aren't—and tries to lighten the mood by saying we should start referring to ourselves as the remainders. All the girls in the class are crowded around him, and I can't shake the pang of jealousy I feel that I'm not by his side. Everyone throws around their theories about the vanishings. Many think that it is magic, that someone is spiriting the houses away.

"Loveness, you're the boffin," Senzeni says. "What do you think is happening?"

I take out a piece of paper from my notebook and write down all the house numbers of the disappeared houses, up through Mai Memory's. Then I take a deep breath and add:

1973. The Dubes.

1996. The Ncubes.

1967. The Makuras.

"I think there is a pattern. I've been trying to figure it out," I say. I hold up my math textbook and point to the section on sequences.

Everyone in class groans.

"It clicked when I wrote down the address numbers. Whether it's magic or math, both have rules, right? It can't be random," I say. "Every sequence has a rule, and the rule helps you to come up with a formula."

"Loveness is still trying to be a teacher's pet even without any teachers here," a girl next to Senzeni says, rolling her eyes. Everyone laughs.

"Shut up, Siphiwe, you can't even do long division at your age," Senzeni says.

The girl crosses her arms and pouts. "The teachers keep striking. How am I supposed to learn anything?" she says.

"You think you can predict which house is next?" Senzeni asks me.

"I think the houses are vanishing in alternating additions and subtractions of prime numbers," I say. "If I'm right, 1973 is next."

Several people gasp. Our teacher lives at that address.

"Whether it's sequences or tikoloshes, I think it's fucked up that nobody cares that our hood is disappearing," Senzeni says.

"Maybe if we lived in Borrowdale Brooke someone would care, but this is Hopley," I say under my breath. No one hears.

When house number 1973 disappears, Mama pours salt outside our front door. She starts frequenting the services of Prophet Madzibaba, who goes on and on about end times and the rapture. Prophet Madzibaba is the go-to prophet to find out who has placed a curse on you. His followers say they witnessed him pull a fish out of a woman's womb. The fish then spoke the names of the relatives who bewitched her. One afternoon, Prophet Madzibaba visits our house in his immaculate white robes which never seem to stain on our street's dusty roads. He gives Mama a two-litre Mazoe Orange Crush bottle filled with water and with two curious-looking rocks floating near the bottom.

"Holy water to protect your family," Prophet Madzibaba says. "Make sure that you pour a cap into everyone's bathwater every day. When it's finished, come for more."

Mama pays the prophet with the money that was meant for my exam registration fees.

As she bids the prophet goodbye, I heat water for my bath on the paraffin stove until bubbles boil on the surface. I pour the water into a bucket and inhale the steam, hoping that the burn will vaporize me, that when I open my eyes I will be reborn to another family in another place better than here. When Mama tries to pour the holy water into my bucket, I slam the Mazoe bottle out of her hands, knocking her backwards. The holy water pours onto the floor. Mama desperately tries to scoop the water up, but it just slips through her hands. With a sneer, I grab a chikorobo from under the kitchen sink and wipe the water away as fast as I can, pushing her back on the floor when she tries to stop me. On her knees she begs me to stop, but I do not stop until the floor is completely dry again. She wails and wails, screams at me for dooming our family. I scream at her for ruining my only ticket out of this place.

We don't speak again for a couple of days as houses 1996 and 1967 disappear.

Baba doesn't seem to care about the vanishings. He hasn't cared about much since losing his job at ZISCO Steel. After the defunct blast furnaces, the countless worker injuries, and the bankruptcy, ZISCO Steel let go of their workforce with no pension. All Baba does these days is drink and sleep. Sometimes he sits out in the sun in front of our house.

"What do you think is happening to the houses?" I ask him.

He turns his head in my direction, eyes unfocused.

"When your beard appears," he sings, slurring his *r*'s, "childhood disappears."

I suck air between my teeth, angry at myself that I would think Baba would say something coherent. Senzeni and his crew walk by my house. He flashes me a smile and yells, "Boffin!"

I leave Baba behind to sing his stupid song.

"House 1967 disappeared today, so you know who's next according to your sequence?" Senzeni says. He does a little bow.

My heart sinks. I've been trying not to think about what this miserable place will be like without Senzeni's antics to make me smile.

"Don't look so sad, boffin," Senzeni says. "People might start to think you care about a tsotsi."

I cross my arms and Senzeni playfully pokes me. "Since I will be a goner come tomorrow," he says, "I'm throwing a big party today. You should come."

"A party? Is that . . . appropriate?" I ask.

"If I'm going to go out, might as well do it with a bang." He twirls the matchstick dangling at the corner of his mouth. "We're going to buy some stuff for the party. Come with us."

Mama's warnings about Senzeni being a no-good tsotsi fly out the window. Why take advice from a woman who used the money supposed to go for my exam registration for holy water?

"Remember how Mr. Moyo always said to us 'maBorn free munonetsa'?" I ask as we walk down to the shops to get the alcohol for the party.

Senzeni sucks on his teeth. Mr. Moyo thought we complained too much, that those born before independence had it harder and that we should be grateful that we were born free.

"Delusional old man, that one. No wonder he was first to disappear," Senzeni says. "What is there to be grateful about? We don't even have a neighborhood anymore. Look at this place."

Senzeni gestures to the eleven vacant lots on either side of the long street. Nothing remains there but fences and dust.

Senzeni hosts his outdoor party at the empty space of 1980, and it spills onto the street. He sets up large speakers that keep all of Hopley up. I have a feeling he wants to be remembered, and this is the only way he knows how. Senzeni blasts "Muchadzoka" by Holy Ten as if wishing the hook of the song, "Muchadzoka zvenyu," were a spell that could bring him back after tomorrow.

My classmates drink hard liquor and gulp down bronco from brown cough syrup bottles until the pain goes away. Senzeni smokes mbanje and offers me the joint. I've always stayed away from alcohol, bronco, and mbanje. My studies have always been the only fuel that I need to keep going. But Mama has taken that away from me. I accept the joint from Senzeni and let the smoke fill my lungs. I cough from the burn, and Senzeni chuckles.

"Slow down, boffin," he says. "I don't want your mother to kill me."

"To hell with her," I say.

"I heard what she did with your exam money," Senzeni says. Nothing in Hopley is a secret. "I'm sorry, boffin."

With enough drink and smoke inside me, I'm lighter, the world is a tapestry of bright colors and music. I count my fingers one by one and laugh like it's the funniest thing in the world. I name each of my fingers after a disappeared household.

"Do you know what I thought the other day, boffin?" Senzeni says, his eyes red. "Since the disappearances are following a pattern, I thought, why doesn't someone stake out the houses at night to see how the houses are disappearing? Me and the boys staked out 1973, 1996, and 1967. Do you know what happened?"

"Poof!" I say, making a gesture with my fingers and laughing.

"Each time it got to midnight during the stakeout," Senzeni says, "we all passed out asleep and woke up with the house gone." He twirls the matchstick in his mouth to distract from the tears gathering in his eyes. "I lost a friend yesterday. He tried to run away. He thought if he went somewhere else, he would survive. But he disappeared too, even though he wasn't inside the house."

I squeeze his shoulder. I don't know what to say, so I ask, "Uchadzoka here?"

Senzeni doesn't answer the question. Instead he reaches into his pocket, takes out an envelope, and hands it to me. I open the envelope, and inside is a stack of crisp bills.

"What is this?"

"Your exam registration fees," Senzeni says. "Before you refuse it, just think of it as a businessman investing in a boffin. Strive Masiyiwa does it all the time." He shrugs and blows smoke rings.

I can't get my racing thoughts to form anything coherent. I want to cry and laugh all at once. I want to toss the money at Senzeni and tell him he is not going anywhere, he can give me the money tomorrow because he isn't going anywhere.

"If anyone can figure out what's happening and stop it, it's you, boffin," Senzeni says.

"What about your own fees?" I ask.

Senzeni chuckles. "You know I'm not about the books. It would be a waste on me. If you can't think of it as an investment, then think of it as hope. This means I believe you will survive this and write your exams at the end of the year."

The music changes to "Kusina Ani." Couples draw closer, beautiful girls twirl and whine on their boyfriends, their dark skin glistening in the moonlight.

"May I have this dance, boffin?" Senzeni says, holding out his hand. I take it and he leads me to the dusty yard we are using as a dance floor. Senzeni puts his arms around my waist and I wrap my hands around his neck. We dance in time with the music. He pulls me closer and softly sings the lyrics in my ears, "Handei tinofara kusina ani. Kusina ani. Kusina ani. Tinozodzoka mangwana."

I pull back and look into his eyes. The regret in his eyes clears the fog of the high, and my anger rises to the surface. Why would he choose tonight of all nights to tell me how he feels about me? Why did he wait until the night before I never see him again?

"Usazondikanganuwewo, boffin" he whispers.

I grieve for him as he dances in front of me. The last I see of Senzeni is him twirling his matchstick searching for warmth in this cold world.

When house number 1998 disappears, an awful silence falls upon the neighborhood. I can't stand being in the house anymore, so I go to my high school's bursar office to pay for my exam registration, just to have something to do.

"You are one of the few people that have registered for exams," the bursar says. "Guess everyone else thinks they will have disappeared by the time exams come."

My head is still heavy from all the drinking and mbanje at Senzeni's party. My heart is heavy too. I'd hoped to see Senzeni's lopsided grin in the morning, and his infuriating matchstick. I longed to hear him call me boffin one more time.

When I walk past his house, I see people who don't live in Hopley gathered around where his house used to be. They are government officials, accompanied by surveyors in white helmets and investors from China. They map out the area and take photographs. It's as if they can't even see us.

Mama runs out of our house and screams at them, "Our houses are disappearing! Our houses are disappearing! Don't you see, don't you see."

She is beaten by riot police with batons and goes back home broken.

Baba's words come hurtling at me. *When your beard appears, childhood disappears.*

Nothing has appeared in Hopley until today.

On the day of house number 1961's disappearance, Mama holds up a Bible and turns to Thessalonians.

"For the Lord himself will come down from heaven, with a loud command, with the voice of the archangel and with the trumpet call of God, and the dead in Christ will rise first," Mama reads out the verse. "After that, we who are still alive and are left will be carried up together with them in the clouds to meet the Lord in the air. And so we will be with the Lord forever."

Mama's evangelism increases daily. I try not to think about our address: 2002.

I grab one of Baba's Chibuku bottles and go out to lie in the dirt as the sun goes down. Senzeni had the right idea about drinking and partying before the end.

"Blessed are the poor in spirit," Mama prays from inside the house, "for theirs is the kingdom of heaven. Blessed are the pure in heart, for they shall see God."

I put my headphones on to block her out. I think about where it all started: 1980. Perhaps everything is tied to 1980. Perhaps I was wrong about the sequence. Perhaps there is an end to the vanishings. Perhaps there is an equation I haven't considered before, a rule I cannot deduce. I play an old video clip in black-and-white of the first president giving a speech at independence. The Union Jack is taken down and our flag is hoisted up, waving freely in the breeze for the first time. I can see so much hope for the future on the faces of the people in the video. I wonder if Mr. Moyo was in that crowd on that day in 1980. I try to imagine how Mr. Moyo felt seeing freedom for the first time, tasting the possibility of raising born-frees. Now that idea is like bad breath and rotting teeth.

I don't know what tomorrow will hold. When our house vanishes at midnight, I wonder where we will wake up. Will it be a better place than Hopley? Perhaps I will open my eyes to the sound of trumpets, to wings carrying me up a beam of light. Perhaps tomorrow I will meet God. Perhaps tomorrow I will inherit the earth.

Acknowledgments

Umuntu ngumuntu ngabantu. A person is only a person through other people. The core teaching of Hunhu/Ubuntu, the humanist philosophy of the Bantu tribes, is the value of community. I would not be here without the people who have breathed life into my dream. I am because we are, and since we are, therefore I am:

For sending me out-of-this-world anecdotes about African magic and mayhem and urging, "You should write a story about this!" my sister, Stacy Ndlovu, who fanned the flames for some of the stories in this collection to burst into life. My father, Stephen Ndlovu, whose stories put me through school. Mama, Glennis Ndlovu, and other African women that I write for.

For your friendship, your brilliance, for Afrofuturist dreaming into existence the impossible, my loves the Voodoonauts cofounders and homies Shingai Njeri Kagunda, LP Kindred, and Hugh "HD" Hunter.

For pandemic writing sessions where early forms of some of these stories were treated with care, the Summer Exhaustion Workshop Crew: Christina Sun, Stephanie Santos, and Marcella Haddad.

For our rant sessions, crit exchanges, and dreaming for better things for our homeland, Rutendo Charleen Chidzodzo.

For your friendship, support, and keeping me fed with jollof rice and zobo, Lola Ojutiku.

For affirming my stories in their early stages, Mukoma wa Ngugi, my undergraduate advisor at Cornell University; my beloved high school teachers Mrs Mangoye, Madame Nyathi, and Mrs B. Dube, for seeing my potential; Lyrae Van Clief-Stefanon, Ernesto Quiñonez, Helena María Viramontes, and J. Robert Lennon, who all taught me valuable craft lessons.

At the University of Massachusetts-Amherst, where many of these stories were written during workshops in the MFA program, my advisor Jeff Parker, for being the best mentor through a crisis and for the encouragement, support, and space to grow; Edie Meidav and Mona Awad, for your kindness and generosity; Ocean Vuong for reminding me to call my younger self into the room and to use intention as my anchor.

Polina Barskova for providing me with a cozy space in California to edit the collection and Buttons the Cat for being an awesome companion.

Institutions that have supported my writing with fellowships including Breadloaf Writers Conference, Tin House, and New York State Summer Writers Institute. The mentors and colleagues I met there such as P. Djéli Clark, Charlie Jane Anders, Annalee Newitz, Bill Campbell, Tobias Buckell, Dinaw Mengestu, Alaya Dawn Johnson, Claire Messud, and many more. Clarion West Writers Workshop for giving me space to teach a course about ngano, a story form from my home country that is the foundation for the stories in this collection.

At the University Press of Kentucky, series editor Lisa Williams for selecting my book, Patrick O'Dowd, Ann Marlowe, and the entire team for handling my first book with care.

And every sarungano and African writer who came before me. Thank you.

Publication Credits

Thank you to all the editors who gave these stories a home in their literary magazines. Stories in this collection appeared in slightly different form in the following publications.

"Red Cloth, White Giraffe," *Fiyah Literary Magazine* 15 (Summer 2020)

"Second Place Is the First Loser," *Kweli Journal*, 2021

"Home Became a Thing with Thorns," *Magazine of Fantasy and Science Fiction*, March/April 2022, as "From This Side of the Rock"

"Swimming with Crocodiles," *Kalahari Review*, September 25, 2019

"Plumtree: True Stories," *Columbia Journal*, 2020

"The Friendship Bench," *Breathe Fiyah*, 2020

"Water Bites Back," *Mermaids Monthly* 9 (September 2021)

"Turtle Heart," *Jellyfish Review*, 2020

"The Soul Would Have No Rainbow," *Africa Risen*, 2022

"When Death Comes to Find You," *Cryptids Emerging*, Volume Silver, 2022

"Drinking from Graveyard Wells," *Black Warrior Review*, 2022

THE UNIVERSITY PRESS OF KENTUCKY
NEW POETRY AND PROSE SERIES

This series features books of contemporary poetry and fiction that exhibit a profound attention to language, strong imagination, formal inventiveness, and awareness of one's literary roots.

SERIES EDITOR: Lisa Williams

ADVISORY BOARD: Camille Dungy, Rebecca Morgan Frank, Silas House, Davis McCombs, and Roger Reeves

Sponsored by Centre College

CENTRE
COLLEGE